D0390468

Prom Kings and Drama Queens

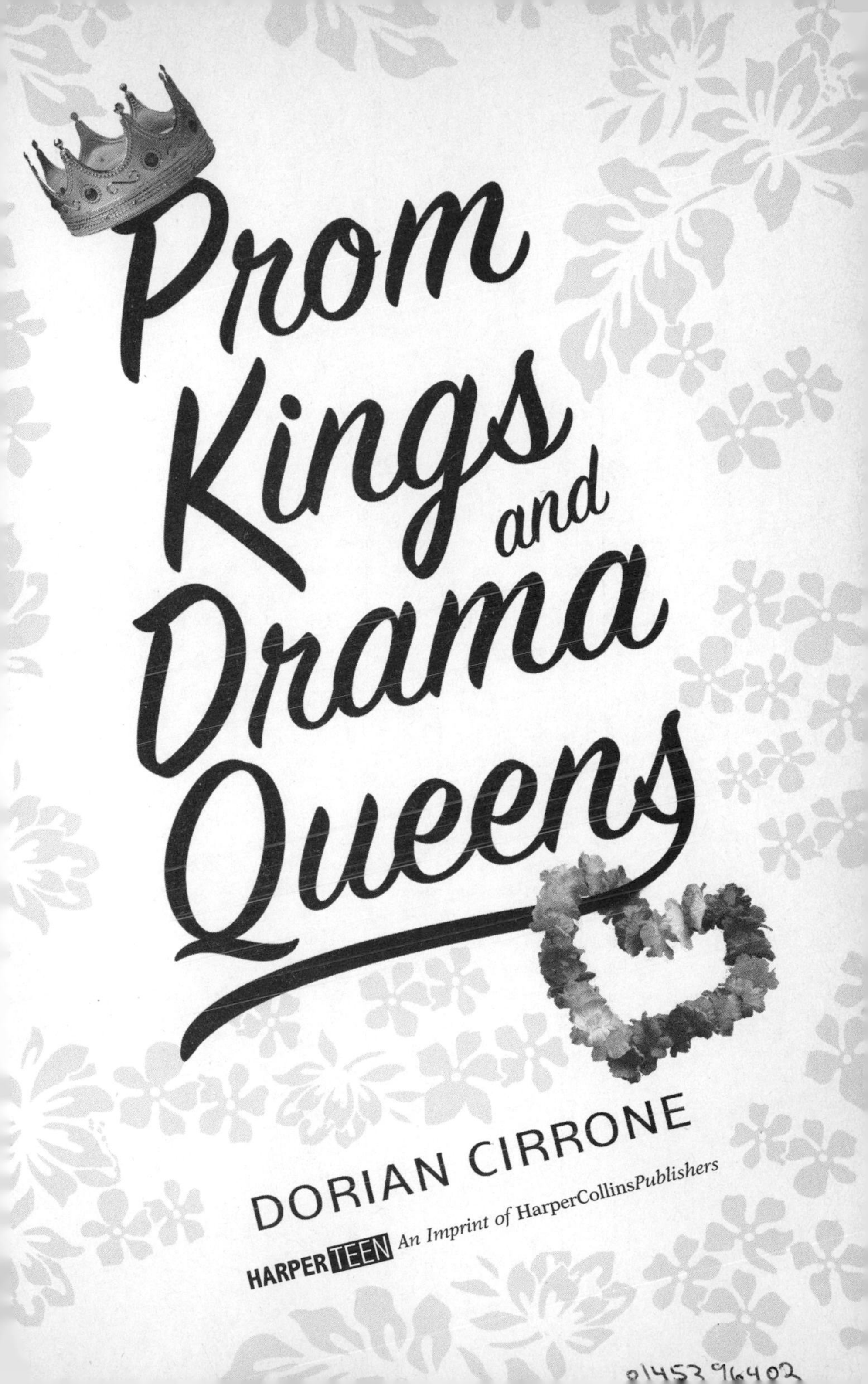

Prom Kings and Drama Queens

DORIAN CIRRONE

HARPERTEEN An Imprint of HarperCollinsPublishers

HarperTeen is an imprint of HarperCollins Publishers.

Prom Kings and Drama Queens

www.harperteen.com

Library of Congress Cataloging-in-Publication Data
Cirrone, Dorian.
Prom kings and drama queens / Dorian Cirrone. — 1st ed.
p. cm.
Summary: When high school junior Emily Bennet is caught between a new relationship with the boy of her dreams and planning an alternative prom with her longtime rival on the student newspaper, it forces her to think about her values and make a difficult decision.
ISBN 978-0-06-114372-4 (trade bdg.)
ISBN 978-0-06-114373-1 (lib. bdg.)
[1. High schools—Fiction. 2. Schools—Fiction. 3. Conduct of life—Fiction. 4. Proms—Fiction. 5. Fort Lauderdale (Fla.)—Fiction.] I. Title.
PZ7.C499Pr 2008 2007020883
[Fic]—dc22 CIP
AC

Typography by Amy Ryan
1 2 3 4 5 6 7 8 9 10
❖
First Edition

For Stephen Koncsol

Prom Kings and Drama Queens

ONE

Emily Poses Little Threat

Junior year was supposed to be all about Brian Harrington, the prom, and becoming editor in chief of the *Crestview Courier*. Instead, it was all about handcuffs, hormones, and headlines.

But in a good way.

Not in a skanky way.

Of course, none of it would have happened if it hadn't been for the summer before eighth grade. That's when twins Brandy and Randy Clausen, my former best friends forever, decided it would be fun to create an I Hate Emily club.

For no apparent reason, except perhaps that I did not get the memo that we were no longer wearing horizontal-striped shirts from the Limited Too, I had been thrust from the inner circle. After an entire eighth grade of being excluded from every shopping trip, sleepover, and party, I vowed I would someday get back at one or both twins.

Around the same time that summer, a hurricane named Emily was in the news. I watched the headlines every day as they shouted: EMILY ROARS ACROSS CARIBBEAN, EMILY BLASTS THROUGH GULF, or, my personal favorite, EMILY ROCKS SOUTH FLORIDA. After reading those headlines each morning for days, I decided two things:

1. I really liked seeing my name in print. And,
2. I wanted to be like that Emily in the headlines.

To take the world by storm.

Not that I wanted to knock over mango trees or whip power lines across the sky like spaghetti. But I wanted to *rock* in my own way.

Somehow.

TWO

Emily Hovers Over Intracoastal Waterway

By the beginning of junior year, I still hadn't figured out a way to show the Clausen twins that they shouldn't have crossed me. Although, there was that time in ninth grade at the Saint Mark's carnival when I took an ill-fated ride on the Zipper. I ended up losing my lunch all over Brandy and Randy, who happened to be sitting downwind.

No one can accuse me of not being an equal opportunity hurler. The twins always said they loved doing *everything* together. And, while it was a fabulous experience watching the two of them scream "Ewwwww" in unison and run to the restroom, it was not the ideal revenge.

I had, however, succeeded in seeing my name in print. I was a feature writer for the *Crestview Courier*, our school newspaper.

But I wanted more.

I wanted to be editor in chief.

And time was running out.

I needed to do two things in order to accomplish my long-held goals:

1. Put the Clausen twins in their place by figuring out what one or both of them held dear and trying to snatch it away. And,
2. Beat out Daniel Cummings, my nemesis and main competition for the editor in chief position on the *Courier*.

Neither of these tasks would be easy.

I'd been writing for the *Crestview Courier* since freshman year, competing with Daniel Cummings. He was a tall, skinny, smart-alecky guy who liked to wear thrift-store T-shirts. He also had a well-read blog called "Cummings and Goings." His most recent entry was an editorial cartoon that pictured a pile of feces with orbiting flies. The caption read STAY IN STOOL. Despite his disrespect for authority, our journalism teacher, Ms. Keenan, seemed to like him.

As for my revenge, after a few months into the school year, it became evident that the one thing Brandy Clausen held dear was Brian Harrington, aka junior class hottie, star athlete, and, as chance would have it, the Boy Next Door.

Really.

He lived next door to me.

Though he and Brandy dated off and on, it didn't seem that he was paying all that much attention to her. She was trying way too hard. The constant flirting and cheering only for him at basketball games were a dead giveaway. But somewhere along the way of my trying to jump in for the ball in a revenge play, an odd thing happened: I fell hopelessly in lust with Brian Harrington.

After observing him for several months, I knew every ripple of his fabulous abs and every bulge of his biceps, as well as the exact location in millimeters of the tiny scar turned dimple under his right eye, which was a slightly lighter blue than his left eye. But it wasn't just his looks. He was different from the other jocks. Nicer. I knew this because every once in a while if he saw my little brother Jon outside, Brian would invite him to shoot a few. Most high school guys wouldn't let a twelve-year-old near the hoop.

Despite the amount of time I had spent studying all things Harrington, and the fact that I lived only yards away, Brian was unaware of my existence as possible girlfriend material.

Finally, in March, all that changed.

Starting with the junior class cruise.

I wasn't sure why the Crestview Prep Student Council had chosen the touristy *Conga Queen* for the class trip. Everyone had already seen the houses along the New River—some of us even lived in them. If you've been in Fort Lauderdale for any length of time, you've probably taken a slew of relatives on a cruise like that. It's practically mandatory, like taking them to the beach—or the flea market for fake jewelry and cheap underwear.

Okay, that probably tells you a little bit more about my family than I should have mentioned.

Anyway, the second my sneakers squeaked across the shiny deck of the *Conga Queen*, I knew something was about to happen. I just didn't know what. I was clenching the railing with one hand and clutching my stomach with the other when I heard Lindsay's voice behind me. "Hey, Em, what's up?"

I turned to face her.

"You don't look so great," she said. "Well, I mean you do look great. I love the outfit and all. But your face, it looks a little green, kind of like the witch in *Wicked*."

Lindsay's the only person I know who could compare seasickness to a Broadway show. But that's why I love her. And I guess I have the Clausen twins to thank for that. If they hadn't blown me off back in middle school, Lindsay and I probably wouldn't have found each other and become such good friends.

I inhaled a huge breath of sea air and looked down at my white capris and navy-striped shirt.

"Are you gonna barf?" Lindsay said.

I shook my head.

"Good, 'cause that would be a one-way ticket to Dorkville."

"Thanks for your support." I plopped onto one of the long wooden benches.

"Sorry," Lindsay said. "But having been there myself for most of middle school, I can tell you it's a place you don't want to be."

While Lindsay and I weren't exactly class pariahs, by the time we reached high school, we were both definitely in touch with our inner nerds. Mainly because of the amount of AP classes we took, but also because of our unnatural relationship to our extracurriculars—me with the newspaper and Lindsay with music. I spent an extra two hours at school every day, working for Ms. Keenan. She'd assigned me the task of researching other high school newspapers all over the country to see how ours could be improved. She was the first teacher to treat me a little bit special and I didn't want to let her down.

Lindsay, who practiced piano *at least* two hours a day, was resident accompanist for the Crestview Choir, which was occasionally pulled out of obscurity to sing the fight song at pep rallies before a big basketball game. Neither of us had gained much acclaim for our efforts, despite the time we put into perfecting our talents. In fact, I was beginning to feel like the only yearbook superlative I'd ever have a chance of winning was Most Likely to Puke.

I stared at the deck, concentrating on a row of ants marching along the wooden floorboards. Lindsay tried to keep my mind off my stomach by giving me a running commentary on the parade of students.

At a school like Crestview Prep you've basically been with the same 150 kids since kindergarten. So by the time you're a junior, you've made the rounds of friendship. You figure out who your real friends are and you're pretty much sick of everyone else. Except, of course . . .

"Oooh, here comes the Boy Next Door," Lindsay whispered.

I peeked up from my ant watching and felt that familiar flutter that a glimpse of him always triggered. Lindsay and I rarely referred to him by his real name. He was always the Boy Next Door.

I'd grown up in an old Fort Lauderdale neighborhood that overlooked the river. In recent years, some of the houses had been renovated by wealthy buyers and made four times their original size. The Harringtons were one of those families. They'd moved in during ninth grade, and in a year, their house became a mansion with a separate guesthouse in back.

Despite the fact that Brian and I attended the same private school, my family's name never appeared on the guest lists for any of the big parties the Harringtons often gave. So it was pretty fair to say that the Boy Next Door could have been the Boy in Idaho and I would have had as much chance of him noticing me.

I watched Brian make his way toward the back of the boat and took a deep breath to calm the jittering.

Bad idea.

The smell of gasoline made me even more seasick. I leaned over the railing.

"We should go see the captain—maybe he can help you," Lindsay said.

I pulled a long strand of hair out of my mouth. "The captain? What can he do?"

"Maybe he's got some kind of drugs you can take."

"Drugs? This from the girl who beat me in the DARE essay contest in fifth grade."

Lindsay laughed. "You're never going to forgive me for that one, are you? I was thinking about some kind of seasickness pills."

I followed Lindsay to the front, eavesdropping on various conversations. One voice stood out among the others. "Do you think it's still considered premarital sex if you don't ever plan on actually marrying the guy?"

I thought it was a joke until I looked over and saw the words were coming out of Randy Clausen's mouth. If anyone else had asked that question, it would have been hilarious. But Randy was serious. And by the look on her face, it seemed she was having a great moral dilemma.

I didn't stick around for the reply. By the time we reached the captain, he had already begun to steer the *Conga Queen* out of her slip. His thick silver hair ruffled in the wind as his head turned from side to side.

Lindsay waited until he was through and the boat was safely into the Intracoastal until she said, "Excuse me."

The captain turned toward us, smiled, and raised his right hand in a salute. "Captain Miguel Velasquez at your service."

Lindsay cleared her throat. "Hi, I'm Lindsay Johnson and this is Emily Bennet. She's not feeling too great."

"Ah, she is seasick?" He pointed to a bench next to the captain's chair.

Lindsay and I sat as he continued. "Let me tell you about seasickness. Your stomach feels this way because your body, it senses the unsteadiness. But your eyes, they do not see it. What have you been looking at?"

I shrugged. "The floor. The ants."

"That is your first mistake," Captain Miguel said. "You must look at the water. If your eyes see the motion, your body will understand what you are feeling inside."

A large boat drove by us, creating whitecaps that rippled and slapped against the side of the *Conga Queen*. The captain pointed to them. "Watch. Then your body will be in harmony with the sea."

At first I thought he'd inhaled a few too many gas fumes from starting the engine so many times. It didn't seem like a great idea to look at the very thing that was making you sick. But after a few minutes of watching the waves, I did begin to feel better.

The night was clear and the air was just cool enough. I stared at the water as we drifted down the river, listening to the other boats beep as they sailed by. Each time we heard a horn, Captain Miguel waved.

"Do you know all those people?" Lindsay asked.

"Most everyone," the captain said. "That is the best part of this job—the people. There are the other captains, the passengers, the fishermen. I wave to them all." He steered the ship between a row of houses. "This is my favorite part," he said, picking up a microphone. "Ladies and gentlemen, we begin our tour."

His voice got lost over the music blaring from the back of the boat, where a DJ played a combination of techno and rap. I looked back and saw Randy and

Brandy dancing with Brian and some of the other basketball players.

The captain pointed out a couple of huge houses that belonged to well-known people—one of them had been a big TV star in the seventies and the other owned a chain of restaurants I'd never been to. I suddenly realized where we were headed when the captain shone a huge light on a familiar house in the distance.

"Hey, that's your house," Lindsay said.

Captain Miguel turned toward me with his eyes so wide his forehead looked like an accordion. "That's *your* house?"

"Um, no, not the one the light's on," I said. "The one next door."

His forehead smoothed out. He seemed deflated for a second. "So you know her, then?"

"Know who?"

"The dancer, the one who—"

Before the captain could finish, he was interrupted by someone yelling, "Hey, Brian, there's your house."

I'd heard from my parents and the neighbors that Brian's grandmother danced in the backyard on Saturday nights for passing ships, but I'd never seen her myself. All the cruises I'd taken along the river had been during the day or on other nights. A huge wooden fence separated our houses, preventing us from seeing into the Harringtons' backyard. I didn't think the show was good enough to risk climbing the fence or springing for a Saturday night cruise. Apparently the captain felt different.

As we got closer, he turned toward Lindsay and me. "Every Saturday, she is out there at nine o'clock without fail." He looked at his watch. "Shhh. It is almost time."

As if on cue, music began blaring from Brian's backyard. A figure dressed in white pants and a sparkly silver top strutted toward the water. The captain adjusted the light so it made a circle in the grass with her standing in the middle. The music in the back of the boat got lower.

Then she began to dance. Her top shimmered as she spun in circles. I recognized the song from the movie *Young Frankenstein*—it was "Puttin' on the Ritz."

"Hey, she's pretty good," Lindsay said.

"No," Captain Miguel said. "She is not just good. She is wonderful!" Then he turned toward me with a strange look. "Do you know her? Do you know her name?"

He sounded kind of like a freshman guy mesmerized by the prospect of meeting the homecoming queen. But could it hurt if I told him her first name? "It's Lily," I said. I wasn't sure how I knew that. I must have heard my mother mention it.

"No one in the neighborhood really knows her. She's

sort of, you know, a couple of tap dances short of a Broadway musical."

"Not her!" Captain Miguel yelled, as if I'd committed blasphemy. "We should all be as crazy as she is. Do you know how much joy she brings to the people who watch her?"

"I'm sorry," I said. "I didn't mean anything. It's just what people say about her."

"What people say," the captain said, shaking his head. "Yes, people say things. But do they go out of their way to make life a little more beautiful for others? That is the trouble. Everyone says you should be this way or that way. What is wrong with being a little different, a little crazy, like . . ." He paused for a second, and then whispered almost reverently, "Lily."

By now Lily had finished her routine and was taking a bow. The captain blew the ship's horn and waved. Lily waved back, bowed again, and blew kisses.

The captain turned the light away from her and pointed the boat toward the Intracoastal. He was quiet for a while, staring out over the wooden steering wheel. Then he turned to me. "Emily," he said. "Do you think you might deliver a message to Lily? From me."

I swallowed. "Um . . ." Would the Harringtons even let me in their house? And what if this Captain Miguel was some kind of perv?

I looked at Lindsay for guidance, but she just

shrugged. "Why not?" she said. "You might score some points with the Boy Next Door."

I turned back to the captain. His pleading eyes were more like a schoolboy's than a stalker's.

"Okay," I said. "I'll deliver the message."

THREE

Emily Delivers on Promise

I pressed the Harringtons' doorbell and then gazed up at the humongous entryway. It was bigger and archier than any doorway I'd ever stood in. I clutched the note in my pocket and examined the wasp nests above me. Great. The sting of humiliation wasn't all I had to worry about.

What was I doing? I mean, really. Look at the entire literary history of love letter delivery.

Romeo and Juliet.

Dead.

Tess of the D'Urbervilles.

Dead.

Cyrano de Bergerac.

Dead. And ugly.

Was there still time to bail? Leave the letter in the mailbox and hope for the best? Wait. I was forgetting the whole reason I was there: the Boy Next Door.

As I thought about the alternate words, Boyfriend Next Door, a shadow appeared behind the etched glass. Before I could see who it was, "Emily?" sounded through the glass.

The door opened and there stood Brian in his gym shorts and no shirt.

Struck speechless for a second, I collected myself and blurted, "How did you know it was me?"

"Video camera. The monitor's in the kitchen."

"Oh," I said. "Very Big Brother."

Brian knitted his brow.

"Nineteen Eighty-four?"

He shook his head. "Before my time."

So he wasn't a literary scholar. But those biceps. My eyes darted back to his face. "How are you doing?"

"Doin' well," he answered, nodding several times. "Doin' well."

The whole "doin' well" thing was a Brian trademark that made girls giggle like they'd just dropped a couple of IQ points. Other guys tried to imitate him, but it never quite worked for anyone else.

After a long pause in which I might have spent a little too much time preoccupied with Brian's abs, he lifted his chin and said, "So what's up?"

"Ummm. Oh yeah," I said, coming out of my six-pack stupor. I hoped Brian's parents weren't in the kitchen watching. I wasn't up for a starring role on Harringtoncam.

I stuck my hand in my pocket and mumbled, "I have this note . . ."

Brian got that look again, as if I was talking about something before his time. "Note?" he said.

"It's for your grandmother."

"Grams?"

Now if that wasn't the most adorable thing ever. Brian Harrington, naked from the waist up, calling his grandmother Grams.

Maybe *adorable* wasn't exactly the right word.

"Why'd you write a note?" Brian said. "You could just come in and talk to her."

"No, no," I explained. "It's not from me. It's from the boat captain. You know, on the cruise last night—in the white jacket and the hat. The captain is apparently a big fan of your grandmother and he asked me if I would deliver this." I held out the note, folded in the shape of a boat.

Brian eyed it suspiciously. "Are you sure this guy isn't a psycho or something?"

I shrugged. "He seemed normal to me. He was totally impressed with your grandmother, said she was a bright spot in his life."

A smile crept across Brian's face as he grunted in surprise. "I guess there are some people who don't think she's a couple inches short of a three-pointer after all."

"Guess not," I said. Was that the right response? Brian opened the door wider and motioned for me to come in. Finally.

The white marble floors looked like you could ice-skate on them. Between that and the ultrahigh ceiling, I felt like I was walking into a mall. Brian guided me through the foyer, then the living room, then another room filled with about a hundred snow globes. When Brian saw the confused look on my face, he explained, "This is the snow globe room. My parents collect them."

I nodded.

"My mom once read that if you collect something, it makes you more memorable to people. When they're on trips and stuff, if they see a snow globe, they'll think of you and buy it as a gift."

"Cool," I said, even though they made me kind of claustrophobic.

Brian shrugged. "It makes it easier for me on holidays." He picked up a globe with a basketball player and ball in midair trapped inside. "This was last Christmas."

We made our way past the kitchen where Brian's

parents were watching a basketball game on TV. Thankfully, Big Brother cam was behind them. They glanced our way as Brian paused and said, "This is Emily-from-next-door."

"Which side?" his mother asked.

Brian pointed in the direction of our house. "Oh," his mother said, "the one with the little boy whose ball keeps going in the yard."

"That's my brother." I laughed nervously. "Nice to see you again," I said, wondering if I'd ever really seen her a first time.

"Emily and I have to work on something for school," Brian said. That was news to me.

His mother nodded and turned back to the game. His father's eyes never left the screen.

I followed Brian through a pair of French doors in the back of the house. I couldn't help but notice that Brian's rear view was right up there with the front in the quality viewing department. "Why'd you tell your mother we were working on a school project?" I asked.

"They'd go into a whole big thing if I told them the truth," he said. "They don't think Grams is wrapped too tight, so they don't like her to have much contact with the outside world."

We stepped onto an open patio with a huge pool and fountain. A small cottage sat across the way. Brian knocked on the side window and then stepped around to open the door.

An older woman in a bright-red robe, wearing a pair of chopsticks in her gray bun sat in front of the television, watching a rerun of *Full House*.

"Brian, dear, how nice of you to visit," she said, "and you brought a friend." She got up and gave Brian a kiss on the cheek, then rubbed off the red lipstick mark she'd made.

"This is Emily-from-next-door."

"It's Bennet," I said a little too loudly. "Emily Bennet."

Lily pointed to the television. "Which one do you like best?" she said.

I looked at Brian for an explanation.

He mouthed the words *Uncle Jesse*.

"Um, Uncle Jesse?"

Lily elbowed Brian and smiled. "She's got good taste."

I breathed a sigh of relief, like I'd just passed a pop quiz.

"And she's so much prettier than that other girlfriend. What's her name? Whiskey? Vodka?"

Brian rolled his eyes. "You know her name's Brandy—and she's not my girlfriend. I've told you a million times, Grams, I *don't* have a girlfriend."

Lily turned toward me and winked. "We'll fix that, won't we?"

I'm sure my face turned as bright as her lipstick. I tried to get out of answering the question by thrusting the origami note forward and almost shouting, "I have a note for you!"

Lily's eyes widened. "Are you one of my fans?"

"Um, oh yes, a fan. Definitely." If that was what it would take to get Brian's attention, I was so going to be a fan. President of the whole freakin' club if necessary. "But it turns out you have a huge fan—even bigger than I am." I dropped the note into her hands. "This is from the captain of the *Conga Queen*."

"Well," Lily said. "I've gotten a few letters in the mailbox, but most are anonymous."

She reached for the note and unfolded it. At the same time, Brian's gym shorts began to play the Crestview fight song.

As he fumbled for his cell, Lily shook her head and frowned.

Brian answered the phone with "Hey." He looked at Lily and me, said, "Be back in a sec," and disappeared onto the patio.

Lily looked me up and down. "So, Emily, do you dance?"

"Not really," I said. "I took some lessons—ballet and tap—in elementary school, but I wasn't very good."

"Nonsense," Lily said, raising her voice. "Anyone can dance."

I laughed. "That's not what the teacher told my mother when she asked why I was always in the back row."

Lily smiled. She didn't seem like the type who would stand for being in the back of anything, except maybe the Harringtons' mansion. "Do you mind if I take a minute to read my fan letter?" she asked.

"No problem," I said, moving to the couch to give her some privacy. "I'll wait here." I sat on the flowered cushion and surveyed the one-room cottage. It was like the anti-Harrington house. Every surface where Brian and his parents lived was adorned with some vase or statue. Lily's place was streamlined and sparse, with no more than two of anything. Two plates, two cups, two chairs around the small kitchen table—a Noah's ark of inanimate objects.

Alone on the couch, I was beginning to think the whole gofer-girl thing had been a big waste of time, when suddenly, Brian's voice streamed through the window screen behind me.

"I don't know," he said. "I don't know if it's worth it."

If what was worth it?

"They're a bunch of losers."

Pause.

"Everyone? All the guys?"

Another pause.

"Okay, I'll meet you in the parking lot next to the

school at seven thirty."

I looked at my watch. *Something* was going on in an hour and a half.

Brian's phone clicked shut, and in a few seconds he was inside the cottage. "So, hey, Grams," he said, nudging her with his elbow. "You've got an admirer, huh?"

For a second I wondered if he was being sarcastic, but I could tell by the look in those baby blue eyes that he was sincere. I wondered if those eyes would ever look at me that way.

Lily tucked the note inside the V-neck of her robe. "Emily," she said. "I'd like to write the captain a response to his lovely note. Will you come back tomorrow to get it?"

Tomorrow? I'd thought this would be a one-time deal. Deliver the note. Get to know Brian better. Then, boom. We're at the prom together.

Well, maybe I'd seen a few too many teen movies. But I really hadn't expected to become a courier between the captain and Lily. That was so middle school—except for the part where they were in their seventies and their acne had cleared up a long time ago.

Brian put his arm around Lily's shoulders. My own shoulders tingled. "Sure," I said. "I'll come after school."

Lily clapped her hands. "That would be wonderful!"

Brian looked at his watch. "Sorry, Grams, gotta go meet the guys."

"You and the guys," she said, shaking her head. "Save some time for your poor old Grams later tonight, okay?"

"Sure thing," Brian said, ushering me out of the cottage.

Lily looked at me and winked once again. What was up with the secret winking language?

"Sorry to rush," Brian said, "but I've got to change."

"Sure." I left through a side door in the wooden fence instead of going through the house again. "So, I guess I'll see you tomorrow then?"

"Yeah," Brian said. "At school."

"I meant after school when I come to pick up the note," I blurted. Oh God, it sounded so desperate.

"Basketball practice," Brian said. "But I'll tell the maid you're coming."

I tried to hide my disappointment. "Okay, then, thanks."

I trudged through the grass to my own house, wondering what had just happened. With only a few words, I had become some kind of matchmaking, letter-delivering go-between for the geriatric set and I wasn't even going to see Brian again.

But there was *some* good news.

Brian Harrington didn't have a girlfriend.

Yet.

FOUR

Emily on Path of Destruction?

I managed to slip past both my parents without enduring an inquisition on where I'd been for the last half hour.

My dad and my brother were playing a game of Jeopardy on the computer. My mother was in the kitchen, slathering a turkey with iodine.

No, it wasn't some kind of death-by-fowl plot to knock off the family with Sunday dinner. She's a food stylist, which means she arranges meals for photographs in magazines and cookbooks. Sometimes she has to go to extremes to make a dish look appetizing. Since we're the fattest country in the world, I'm not sure why this is necessary.

"Potent Potables for two hundred," my father yelled, as I passed the study and climbed the stairs. My dad's an accountant, or as my mom would say, a "numbers guy." But he and my brother seem to bond best over games like Jeopardy and Wheel of Fortune.

"Computer Game Show Geeks for five hundred," I shouted, before closing my bedroom door. The second I sat on the bed, the phone rang.

"He-llo," Lindsay said. "And when were you planning on filling me in on the Harrington caper?"

"Caper?" I said. "What are you, fifty years old?"

"You know what I mean. Did you get to see Brian?"

I leaned back on my pillow. "Not only did I see him, I saw him sans shirt."

"And . . . ?"

"And . . . it was a pretty fine sight."

"That's it?" Lindsay said. "I want details."

I hesitated. "Well . . . I think he shaves his chest hair. And—"

"Ewww," Lindsay interrupted. "Way too much information. I meant details about the interaction, not the anatomy."

"Oh, okay. Short version: Knocked on the door. Apparently made an appearance on the Harrington Home Security Network. Met the parents—sort of. Met Grams and—"

Lindsay interrupted again. "Grams?"

"That's what Brian calls his grandmother. Cute, huh? Anyway, I gave her the note. She read it, stuck it in her bra, and told me to come back tomorrow to pick up a response for Captain Miguel."

"A response? Are you going back?"

"I guess so," I said. "She's sort of intimidating—in an old lady kind of way."

"Maybe you could start an online dating service for old people," Lindsay said. "You know, like squeeze-a-geezer dot com."

"Very funny," I said, trying to get the visual out of my head and replace it with one of Brian.

"So in addition to your newfound matchmaking avocation, did you learn anything about the world of Brian Harrington?"

"Well, he apparently doesn't consider Brandy Clausen his girlfriend—he told his grandmother he didn't have a girlfriend."

"Whoa, that's major," Lindsay said. "What else?"

"Not too much," I said, "just that his parents seem to have a thing for snow globes. They've got a whole room for them."

"What?" Lindsay's voice rose an octave. "I'm sleeping in a room that triples as a den *and* my mother's office, and they've got a whole room devoted to a bunch of knickknacks?"

It annoyed Lindsay when she saw people spend a lot

of money on stuff she thought was useless. Her parents were divorced, and her mother struggled to pay all the bills. Luckily Lindsay was on scholarship at Crestview.

I figured I'd better change the subject before she decided to be annoyed at Brian, too. In case my master plan worked and I lucked out in the crush department, I couldn't have my best friend hating my boyfriend. "Anyway," I said, "something weird happened."

"What?" Lindsay said. "Did they have a whole room for Precious Moments figures, too?"

"No," I continued, ignoring her sarcasm. "Brian got a phone call while I was there. He went outside to talk, like he didn't want anyone to hear."

"Do you think it was Brandy?"

"It wasn't that kind of whispering. It was more like secret-plan whispering."

"What kind of plan?"

"Beats me," I said. "All I know is that a bunch of kids are all meeting tonight at seven thirty in the parking lot by school."

"How did you hear that part?"

"He said it right before he walked back into his grandmother's cottage."

"You mean they have a whole room for snow globes in that big house, but his grandmother has to live in a cottage?"

"I don't know," I said. "I think she likes it there.

Besides, I don't think living with the Harringtons is any day at the spa. But that isn't the point. The point is that Brian Harrington is up to something with someone and I want to know what it is."

There was a pause on the other end. "You could follow him," Lindsay said.

"And add stalking to my list of extracurriculars? No, thank you. I think I'll stick to writing for the *Crestview Courier*."

"Think of it this way," Lindsay said. "You're an investigative reporter. You'll be investigating a secret plan made by one of the most popular guys in school. It's practically Pulitzer material."

"Right," I said. "What if they're just getting together for dinner? 'Girl reporter cracks fast-food-eating ring.'"

"Do you really think he'd keep it a secret if that's all they were doing?" Lindsay said. "You've got to follow him. . . . You know you want to."

Lindsay was right. As soon as I conjured that swoon-worthy smile and those eyes, I wanted to follow Brian Harrington anywhere.

But, hey, I wasn't just a stalker. I was a journalist, too. And once I thought about it, Brian *had* ushered me out of the house awfully fast. Something was definitely going on. It might not be a prize-winning journalism piece, but, yeah, I wanted to know what Brian was up to. Maybe I *would* get a story out of it. "You want to come with me?" I asked.

"Gotta practice," Lindsay said.

I groaned. Lindsay's practicing had interfered with a good 50 percent of our plans since we met. Her diligence made me a better student, though. I don't think I'd have worked nearly as hard on the school paper if it hadn't been for her example.

"You can go by yourself. It's not like it's midnight or anything," Lindsay said.

"But what if I get kidnapped and put to work in a slave-wage factory making midriff shirts for the rich and famous?"

Lindsay laughed. "Send me a shirt."

"No, really. You've gotta come with me. It's not fair. You're the one who talked me into it. And, who knows, maybe it'll be my chance to scoop Daniel Cummings. If I get a great story, I'll have an edge on the editor position for next year."

"And what do I get?"

"You get to be best friends with the editor of the school newspaper," I said. "Think of the power."

"Hmm," Lindsay said. "Can I get on the front page?"

"It's a possibility."

"Well, all right. But I'm mostly doing this to be a good friend. So you and Brian can get married and have babies together."

"Whoa, stop planning the shower and get ready."

I hung up the phone and darted down the stairs. When I got to the kitchen my mom was still working on the poultry photo shoot.

She looked up at me and sighed. "This turkey is so unphotogenic."

"Why don't you take it to Glamour Shots?" I said, opening the refrigerator door.

She gave me one of her that-is-not-helpful looks.

Without really examining the refrigerator's contents, I said, "Do you mind if I go out and get something to eat with Lindsay? Especially since you're obviously preoccupied with the bird-beautification project." A little guilt never hurt.

"Sure," she said. She stuck a pin on the underside of a turkey leg. "We're just getting pizza anyway. But do me a favor; pick up some more iodine on the way home."

"Okay," I said, "but I might be a little late. There's a group studying together after dinner."

"Just call if you'll be later than eleven." She leaned over and kissed me on the cheek.

"Good luck with the turkey makeover." I grabbed my keys from the kitchen counter.

I slid behind the steering wheel. Technically, I hadn't lied. I probably would get something to eat. And I was sure there was a group *somewhere* that was studying after dinner. I just wasn't in it.

I looked at the Harrington house and then at my watch. Six thirty. I had enough time to pick up Lindsay *and* make myself an honest woman by grabbing dinner before Brian and whoever got to the meeting place. I figured we'd get sandwiches and spy from the sub shop next to the school parking lot.

Lindsay was waiting outside when I pulled up in front of her house.

"Got your spy camera?" I said.

"What?"

"Just kidding."

"You better be. You know I'm only doing this so at least one of us has a date to the prom," Lindsay said.

We rolled into the drive-thru line and ordered tuna subs with provolone and then pulled into a spot where we could get a good view of the rendezvous point. The parking lot was an unpaved piece of land outside the Crestview gates.

I took a bite of my sandwich and looked at Lindsay.

"So where's this secret meeting?" she said.

I looked down at my reporter's notebook and suddenly felt a pang. Did I honestly think there would be some front-page story potential here? Or was I just fruitlessly following Brian around?

Just when I was going to suggest we leave, we heard the crunch of tires. We slunk down in the seat—not that anyone Brian was friends with would even look over at my Saturn. It wasn't exactly the kind of car that cool kids covet.

A few minutes later another car drove in, then another. They were the same ones always parked in front of Brian's house. Basketball players' cars. Was it a practice? Why whisper about that? When Brian's convertible finally rolled over the rocks and into a space, everyone got out of their cars and into a huddle. After a few minutes, they broke apart, got back into their cars, and started their engines in unison. Teamwork.

I swallowed my last bit of sub and watched as the first car, a red BMW, left the lot. "Last chance," I said. "Follow or bail?"

Lindsay crinkled her sub wrapper. "We've come this far."

I started my engine and inched out of the parking lot. "Okay," I said. "Remember, we're following a black SUV with the license plate HOOP29."

"Got it," Lindsay said.

I was a reporter on a story.

A girl on a mission. Searching for truth.

Ahh. Who was I kidding?

I was a girl following the crush next door.

FIVE

Emily a Danger to Tall Trees?

"Faster," Lindsay said. "You're losing them."

I glanced to the side of the road for a speed limit posted. No sign. My chocolate Typhoon was dripping into the cup holder. I turned up the AC so it wouldn't melt anymore.

"Pedal to the metal," Lindsay shouted.

"Where'd you pick that one up?" I said. "During your many other car chases between piano lessons?" I took a deep breath and pressed my foot on the gas a little harder. The car smelled like onions. My heart rate climbed along with the speedometer, and my adrenaline revved. I was just beginning to picture myself as the heroine of an adventure movie when Lindsay brought me back to reality.

"Light!" she screamed. "Yellow light! Up ahead. We could lose them."

I watched the first car zoom through. Then the second and third. As the light was about to turn red, the SUV jammed on the brakes, causing me to do the same. Lindsay caught my Typhoon as it lurched out of the holder. "That was close," she said, shoving the cup at me.

I slurped several times and then shoveled the rest of it into my mouth with the plastic spoon. The light turned green. "Ohhh, brain freeze, brain freeze!" I grabbed my forehead and hit the gas.

"Why does something so good have to hurt?" Lindsay said.

I shook my head and glued my eyes on the SUV in front of me. He didn't speed up to catch the others. Apparently, they all knew the meeting place. That was a relief. I didn't know how I would explain getting a speeding ticket on a road that wasn't on the way to Lindsay's. "What road is this anyway?"

"It's Dixie," Lindsay said. "I take it to visit my dad."

"So where do you think they're going?"

"Probably not my dad's."

"Thanks for the tip." I couldn't help but wonder if the whole girl reporter-slash-detective thing was worth it. I had homework waiting for me. I was wasting gas.

And Brian's car had been out of sight for about five minutes. Not that that was the reason I'd joined the caravan.

No. I was still trying to convince myself I was following a lead. I didn't know what it was yet. But wasn't that how all good news stories started out?

At the next light, the car in front of me turned right onto a narrow two-lane street. "Where *are* we?" I said. The darkened road wasn't deserted—a few houses lined the street on either side. But it was definitely unfamiliar territory.

"Look," Lindsay said, "they're stopping. It looks like a field and some buildings."

We got closer and I saw the huge sign: SAINT BARTHOLOMEW'S CATHOLIC SCHOOL. "Aren't they the ones that beat us in basketball every year?"

"It's starting to make sense now," Lindsay said. "Oh God, I hope it's not a gang war."

"Gang war? Do you honestly think those guys look the type? I mean, they're not all hotties like Brian, but, c'mon, I don't think any of them want their faces punched in—or even their clothes messed up."

I held back and pulled over in front of one of the houses. I rolled down the windows halfway and switched off the ignition. We watched as the four cars parked outside the gates near a massive tree.

Lindsay and I ducked down and peered over the

dashboard. The tallest guy on the team, Luis Rivera, got out first, and the rest gathered around the trunk of Luis's car.

"What are they doing?" Lindsay whispered. "I've seen a lot of scary movies. Nothing good is ever in the trunk."

I laughed, even though my heart was starting to pound a little. "Look who we're talking about here. They're not criminals."

"Oh really?" Lindsay said. "Aren't these the same guys who have fake IDs and get drunk at parties?"

"Chill out," I said. "Getting wasted at a party is not equivalent to body parts in a trunk."

Luis and a guy named Austin leaned forward as the others gave them some room.

Lindsay was tapping her fingers on the dashboard like it was a piano. I knew she was wishing I'd never talked her into this. Luis hoisted something out of the trunk. He faltered as he straightened up and stepped back.

Lindsay seemed to be tapping out a whole concerto on the dashboard. "Oh my God," she whispered. "I knew it. Look how he lost his balance. It's heavy. It's dead. It's a heavy dead thing in the trunk."

"What heavy dead thing would have anything to do with Saint Bart's?" I whispered.

"What's their mascot?" Lindsay shot back.

"Bulldog," I said.

Lindsay gasped. "That's it. They killed a bulldog. Like in *The Godfather*."

"They killed a bulldog in *The Godfather*?" I'd seen all three movies with my parents during one of our video marathon weekends, but had fallen asleep during some of the parts. I imagined Al Pacino putting out a hit on a bulldog, but it definitely didn't seem right.

"It was a horse head in a bed. To send a message," Lindsay said. "Don't you get it? A dead bulldog would send a message that we're going to whip their basketball team this year."

"Canine corpse equals county championship? I don't think so. Besides, where would they get a dead bulldog, anyway?"

"Luis," Lindsay said. "His father's a veterinarian."

I groaned. "My uncle's a doctor, but he doesn't leave corpses around the house for my cousins to use for revenge schemes."

"*Shh, shh,*" Lindsay said. "They're moving."

As Luis stepped away from the group, we saw it. Even in the dark there was no mistaking what it was. Lindsay gasped again. "It's a—"

"*Texas Chainsaw Massacre* anyone?"

We both stifled screams and spun toward the voice. Daniel Cummings's chin was resting on my driver's-side window.

"What are you doing here?" I demanded through clenched teeth.

He grinned. "Same thing you're doing here. Unless I'm wrong and you and your little sidekick are working as lookouts for the Crestview Cretins."

"Funny," I said. "You mean you knew about this ahead of time? How?"

"I have my sources," Daniel said.

At this point, I was afraid Lindsay was going to tap a hole in my dashboard. "You knew and you didn't try to stop them?" I said.

"Stop them from doing what? They haven't done anything yet."

"Yet!" Lindsay said. "If you know something, Daniel, you better speak up before we're all accessories to a homicide."

"Homicide!" Daniel laughed. "More like oakicide."

"What?" Lindsay and I said in unison.

"They're going to try to cut down that tree."

"What for?" I said.

"Because it's the pride and joy of Saint Bart's. It's the largest oak tree in the city, and it's been there since before the school was founded back in the forties."

"So?" I said.

"So who says a bunch of egotistical jerks have to have a good reason for doing something stupid?" Daniel said. "It's a macho sports thing. The Bulldogs made some threat about kicking our butts on the court, and next thing you know . . . Saint Bart's Chainsaw Massacre."

"How do you know all this?" I said.

"My cousin goes to Saint Bart's. That's how I found out about the tree. I didn't know the whole plan till now. I knew the team was meeting here, but I didn't know why."

I leaned back in the seat. "What do we do now that we know?"

Daniel shrugged.

I imagined running up to the team and yelling, "Stop, stop! You mustn't hurt the tree." That was one way to ensure Brian Harrington would think I was a big dork.

"We *are* reporters," Daniel said. "We might as well get a closer look so we can at least see what's going on."

I glanced at Lindsay, who was glaring at the group now huddled around the famous oak tree that was soon to be the famous dead oak tree. "Wanna come?"

She shook her head without shifting her eyes a millimeter. I gently opened the car door, stepped out, and then closed it with a slight click. "Be back soon."

Daniel and I inched forward, hiding behind neighboring cars as we headed toward the tree. I listened to the rhythm of our almost silent steps and tried to remember why I was doing this: I'm a reporter. I don't want Daniel Cummings to get the story and not me. But one big reason not to do it kept crowding into my head: I could get caught. I could get caught. I could get caught.

Then again, I couldn't walk away now. Daniel and I got as close as we could and hid behind an SUV about thirty feet from the guys. We could hear them laughing.

"We are definitely gonna show those Saint Bart's guys who's boss," a voice said.

"I don't know. It's a pretty nice tree," another voice said. I recognized it as Brian's. My heart swelled inside my chest. He wasn't like those other guys after all.

"Are you kidding me?" Luis said. "We got this far. We're doin' it."

Another voice: "Yeah, let 'er rip!"

The sound of a chain saw starting up suddenly cut through the quiet, drowning out the music of chirping crickets. I winced as the saw clunked against the trunk. They were really going through with it.

I turned to Daniel. "Should we stop them?"

"Do you really think they'd listen to us?" Daniel answered. "Besides, reporters don't get involved. They just report the news."

"Not when something bad is happening," I whispered frantically.

Daniel stuffed his hands in his pockets and hunched over. "All those journalists that cover stories about things like child slave trade in this country . . . they just tell the stories. It's someone else's job to fix it."

Images of emaciated children loaded into the backs of trucks flashed before me. "So what do we do about this? Report it in the school paper? By then it'll be too late for anyone to do anything."

"Yeah, you're right, but—"

Suddenly Luis Rivera let out a string of obscenities like I'd never heard and a siren sounded from down the block. In unison, the guys raced to their cars and started the ignitions like it was the Indy 500. One at a time, as if they'd planned it, they screeched out into the street and disappeared.

I froze as the siren came closer. "What do we do?"

Daniel's face turned blue. Then not blue. Then blue again. The cop car with its flashing light was speeding toward us.

Before Daniel could answer the question, a large hand clamped down on my shoulder and a deep voice growled, "What do you think you're doing here?"

SIX

Emily's Strength Curtailed

The next thing I felt was a pair of lips on mine. No. Make that a pair of lips practically trying to suck mine off. It was too dark to see, but I figured there was a good chance they belonged to Daniel and not the random guy who had his hand on my shoulder.

Either way.

Gross.

"Ewww," I shouted, pushing Daniel off me. "What are you doing?"

He stomped hard on my foot and grabbed my hand. I was too stunned to react.

"I'm sorry, sir," Daniel said quickly. "We were just taking a walk and, uh, well, you know, Emily's my girlfriend, so we stopped for a second to, you know . . ."

Good one, Emily, think before blurting. "Um, yes," I added, "Daniel's my, um, boy . . . friend." The word was a little hard to get out.

Just as Daniel opened up his mouth again, a light suddenly illuminated his face. I hoped it was a comet crashing to Earth.

"What's going on here?" the cop said, turning the light toward me.

The burly guy, whose voice matched his large, naked, hairy chest, had finally taken his hand off my shoulder. "I caught these two out here watching a bunch of guys at the school. They must be gang members or somethin'—the others got away."

The cop looked at Daniel's khaki pants and T-shirt with the big basketball that read I HAD A BALL AT JEREMY'S BAR MITZVAH.

"Gang member, huh?" the policeman said. He turned back to me. "And what are you doing here?"

"She's my girlfriend," Daniel said.

There was that word again.

"We were just taking a walk," he added.

"Where's your ID?" the cop demanded.

Daniel fumbled for his wallet while I froze. I'd left my purse in the car with Lindsay. I couldn't go back and get it without getting her in trouble, too. She'd be grounded until the end of college if her mother ever found out Lindsay had lied about where she was going. "I left mine at home," I said.

Daniel picked up the cue. "It's okay. She drove with me." He produced his driver's license and held it under the flashlight.

"So," the cop said, "you live in Lauderdale?" He turned back to me. "And what about you, Miss No ID? Where do you live?"

I hesitated. There was no way I could say I lived in the neighborhood of St. Bart's. He'd ask me where, and then I'd be in big trouble. "Um, Fort Lauderdale."

"So the two of you are from Lauderdale, but you had to come all the way up here to this block for a romantic stroll? And, coincidentally, I get a call at the same time that there's an incident of vandalism going on at Saint Bart's." He paused for a second, and then added. "Do I have *dumb ass* written on my forehead?"

He turned to the shirtless guy. "How many of them were there altogether?"

"Countin' these two, eleven," he said. "The others were all big guys. They were over by that tree makin' a racket with a chain saw."

The policeman grabbed Daniel's elbow. "How 'bout we take another stroll."

Mr. Neighborhood Crime Watch tried to grab my elbow, but I jerked it away.

The cop shone the light onto the tree and walked

around it until he found the evidence he was looking for—a big jaggedy slash across the lower trunk. It looked like a giant, scary smile.

"What do you two know about this?" the cop said.

Daniel shrugged.

"And don't give me that romantic stroll crap. It's no coincidence you two were out here at the same time some guys were trying to cut down this tree." He pressed his fingers into the indentation the chain saw had made and laughed. "Paul Bunyan couldn't cut down this sucker. You're lucky those idiots didn't know what they were doing, or you'd be in real trouble."

I wondered what kind of trouble we were in now. Was it fake trouble? Did that mean he'd let us go?

The cop turned toward me. "Now, let's see. What do *you* know about this?" It suddenly occurred to me—it might not seem like "real" trouble in the world of cops, but in my world, I was in deep Saint Bart's Bulldog doo. My heart beat so fast it almost vibrated like Luis's chain saw. Think fast, Emily.

"We're reporters," I blurted. "We heard a rumor about something going on at Saint Bart's tonight." What was that phrase? The truth can set you free. Boy, did I hope whoever said that knew what he was talking about.

"That's right," Daniel said. "But we didn't know what it was."

"Where'd you hear the rumor?" the cop asked.

I shrugged, remembering the phone call outside the cottage at Brian's house. "Around," I mumbled. Could a half truth also set you free?

"You?" the cop said, turning to Daniel.

"School," he said.

The cop put his hand on his gun. "You heard a rumor at school, but you didn't know what was goin' down?"

"Yes, sir," Daniel said.

The cop turned to me. "Who were the guys with the chain saw?"

Oh my God. Truth? Lie? Truth? Lie?

I heard the words "I don't know" escape from my lips.

"None of them looked familiar?" the cop said.

I stared at the huge roots that spread out from the bottom of the oak tree. "It was dark," I said.

"And it's a big school," Daniel added. "We don't know everyone."

I breathed a sigh of relief. Daniel was backing me up. We were reporters covering a potential crime, but we never got to see the culprits. End of story.

I looked at my watch. Nine forty-five. Plenty of time to get home before curfew.

The cop nodded slowly. It seemed like he was just about to let us go, but then he said, "Let's take another stroll—over to the squad car."

Daniel and I exchanged fleeting looks of terror. My heart thumped about thirty times with each step.

At the squad car, the cop turned to us. "You see," he said, "a crime's been committed here. Since you two don't seem to recall who the members of the chain saw gang were, I'm gonna have to take you in on suspicion of covering up that crime."

I swallowed hard and used all my energy to not cry. Take you in. Take you in. The words got louder with each obsessive repetition in my brain.

Burly guy stood over us like the dog in the Crime Watch posters as the cop reached into the squad car. The next thing I saw was the glint of silver in the moonlight.

"Hands behind your backs, both of you." The cop's words mingled with the clink of the handcuffs as he slapped a pair across Daniel's wrists first and then mine. He opened the back door of the car and motioned for us to get in as he recited our rights. Daniel crouched so his head wouldn't hit the roof and slid across the seat. I followed.

There was no fooling myself now. This was "real" trouble.

I stared at the floor as the cop thanked the bare-chested guy for being such a good neighbor. Yeah, right.

As we rode past my car, I saw an empty passenger seat. Lindsay was probably scrunched down so low, she had to tap her fingers on the floor. I figured she was on her fourth concerto by now.

I looked up at the seat belt to the left and thought about how my mom would kill me if she knew I wasn't wearing it. Then I shivered at the irony.

I leaned forward and tried to ignore the sick feeling in my stomach. My wrists ached already. A searing pain shot through them when I forgot and leaned back in the seat.

When we got to the police station and they took off the handcuffs, my relief was short-lived. Daniel and I were taken by another policeman into a large room with a big table and metal chairs. He sat us next to each other. Then he asked us our full names and a whole bunch of questions: address, phone number, height, weight, tattoos . . .

I looked at a tattooless Daniel, who was five foot ten and weighed 130. Could I get in even more trouble if I shaved a couple of pounds off my weight? I was only five foot five and weighed almost as much as he did. That kind of information was never supposed to be public.

The room was freezing and every word we uttered seemed to echo a thousand times. When the cop was finished, Daniel and I sat motionless without saying a word to each other. I'd seen enough shows on TV to know there might be a two-way mirror or a tape recorder or something.

The only sound in the room was Daniel's heel bouncing up and down on the tile floor.

My life as I had formerly known it flashed through my head. I'd wanted Brian Harrington to notice me and now the whole school was going to notice me. But not in a good way. In a skanky ex-con kind of way.

I looked at my watch. Ten forty-five. Making curfew was just a fantasy now. I wasn't sure what would happen next, but I was pretty sure it would involve me, my parents, and a whole lot of screaming.

After the longest half hour of my life, my mom and dad showed up. But, strangely, there was not a whole lot of screaming. There was, however, a lot of cold silence.

Daniel and I were told to go up to the front desk. The only time my parents spoke was to talk to the policeman in charge.

It was different when Daniel's parents saw him. His mom called out his name really loud, rushed over to him, and kissed him on the head. His dad, who was a lawyer, began talking in a booming voice with a whole lot of legal terms I didn't understand. It reminded me of a cartoon I once saw with a man talking to his dog, but all the dog hears is "Blah, blah, blah, Ginger, blah, blah,

blah." The only words I really heard were "let them go."

The next thing I knew, I was in the back of my dad's car. This time I put on the seat belt.

Silence.

That is until we left the parking lot.

"Emily! What were you thinking?" That was my father.

"We were worried sick when we got the call." That was my mother.

"I'm sorry. I'm sorry." I said. My eyes stung as tears spilled out. "I'll never do anything like that again. I'm so sorry."

"Do you have any idea what the consequences of this could be?" My father again.

"You've got a lot of explaining to do." Back to Mom, whose voice was verging on hysterical.

Silence.

"Well?" Both of them at the same time.

"I didn't think I was doing anything wrong," I said. "I just wanted to get a scoop for the school newspaper. I thought I'd be sure to get the editor job next year if I could show what kind of investigative reporter I was."

"Excuse me," my mother said. "Lying to me about where you were going wasn't wrong?"

I hesitated. "Well, that part was wrong. But really it was all because I wanted to get the story." Again, maybe that wasn't the whole truth. There was the tiny little part about having a major crush on Brian Harrington and how I'd follow him anywhere just to find out more about him.

I tried to impress upon my parents how I'd thought getting the story, and subsequently the editor position, would have really helped me get into a good college, but they suddenly got way past wanting to hear more of my side of the story.

Both went on and on about what a stupid thing I'd done and thank goodness Lindsay had called them about the car. And who did Daniel and I think we were, anyway, Woodward and Bernstein?

I didn't think it was a good time to tell them that Daniel and I were nothing like Woodward and Bernstein because Daniel and I were not partners in any sense of the word.

It was late by the time we got home. My parents sent me up to my room and told me to get a good night's sleep because there was no way I was missing school the next day.

I took a quick shower and smeared some soap over my lips where Daniel had kissed me. He was definitely not the person I'd hoped to lock lips with that night.

SEVEN

Emily's Power Wanes

Monday morning. The morning after. I'd heard that phrase used after an evening of excess and decadence. But the only thing I'd done that came close to debauchery was the whole handcuff thing, and that was definitely not a kinky experience. Nope. No kink at all. Unless you threw in Daniel's surprise smoocheroo, which, eww, I was trying to forget.

After the parental Lecture on Lying, Part *Deux* over my cinnamon oatmeal, I was almost grateful to be in school. To be in homeroom with Ms. Davidson, who was also my third-year Latin teacher and all-time favorite. My gratitude, however, was short-lived. After the pledge, someone showed up at the door with a request for my presence in the principal's office. Fortunately, Ms. Davidson didn't make a scene when she handed me the note. But I could tell she was dying to know what was up.

Wait until she finds out: I came, I saw, I almost got arrested. *Veni, vidi* . . . crap. *Getting arrested* hadn't come up in Latin class yet.

Ordinarily I'd find the principal's office amusing—Ms. Burns's tiny frame tottering on four-inch heels that were supposed to make her look more authoritarian. The giant oil painting of her on the wall. The embroidered pillow on her seat that read NO CHILD LEFT BEHIND that she put her, uh, behind on. But as Daniel and I took the two seats across from her, all I could do was sit and tremble.

Ms. Burns pursed her lips, then spoke. "I received an interesting phone call this morning from the principal at Saint Bart's. It seems a group of boys tried to cut down a landmark oak tree in front of the school." She punctuated the sentence with more pursing.

There was a long silence. The only sound was Daniel's heel bouncing up and down on the tile floor—again.

Would we be able to stick to our original story—that it was too dark and Daniel and I weren't able to see who was there? Or would she force the truth out of us with threats of expulsion or black marks on our permanent records? My pulse kept time with Daniel's foot as the blood rushed to my head and began to throb at my temples.

Ms. Burns folded her hands on top of her dark wooden desk. “The vandals apparently were frightened by the police and got away before any real damage was done. But you two were not as fortunate. In fact, if you weren’t so-called *covering* the event for the school newspaper, the whole connection to Crestview Prep might have gone unnoticed.”

Wait a minute. What exactly was she saying? That Daniel and I were the ones to blame?

Ms. Burns shifted on her pillow. “I’ve spoken to Dean Anderson and your parents, and we’ve all agreed that it’s best to forget the whole incident.”

Again. *Hello*? Was I hearing right? She actually didn’t *want* to know the identities of the chain saw gang?

She turned toward Daniel. “I believe your father worked it out that there would be no charges against either of you if you agreed to perform community service.”

I vaguely remembered hearing Mr. Cummings say something about that at the police station. In between trying to keep all my bodily functions from releasing at once.

“You may count those hours toward your school service requirement,” she added, “as long as there is absolutely no gossip about this incident at all.” She leaned forward so that I could smell her stale coffee breath. "Are we clear on this?"

Daniel and I uttered low yesses in unison.

"You may go to class now," she commanded, without getting up.

Daniel and I fumbled with our backpacks in silence and took the walk of shame from the chairs to the door. Thankfully, none of the secretaries seemed interested in us as we slunk past their desks into the main hall.

"What was that?" I said. "Did I understand right?"

Daniel shrugged. "Depends."

I adjusted the weight of my backpack. "On what?"

"On what you think she said." He walked away from the office door and down the hall toward a big sign that read BLUDGEON THE BULLDOGS.

"It sounded to me like she was telling us it was a *good* thing that we didn't tell who we saw and we should keep it that way."

Daniel snickered. "What happens at Crestview stays at Crestview."

"Huh?" I said.

He snickered again. "How long have you been going to this school?"

I glared at him. "Since elementary school. Same as you."

"And you still haven't figured it out? Basketball reigns supreme. The team keeps winning. The school gets more name recognition. That means more rich parents can brag at the beach club. If the team gets booted out of the finals, good-bye bragging rights and good-bye big-time benefactors."

I thought for a second. "So it's like we're taking one for the team."

Daniel laughed, and for the first time I noticed he had really straight teeth. "If you want to look at it that way, go ahead."

The stench of Meatloaf Monday wafted from the cafeteria as we paused in front of the school trophy case. "Takin' one for the team," I said. "Pretty cool."

"Yeah," Daniel said. "Think we can get an athletic scholarship now?"

I caught the sardonic tone and didn't respond. We continued walking down the deserted hallway. Several teachers' voices penetrated their classroom doors and merged into one disjointed lecture. "So why did you lie about not knowing who was there?" I asked, conscious that it was the first time either of us had used the *L* word.

Daniel shrugged. "After you told the cops you didn't see who it was, I realized you were right. I kept quiet for the same reason you did."

I was pretty sure Daniel did *not* mean he also had a crush on Brian Harrington and that he did *not* want to jump Brian's bones. But before I could think of a clever way to ask what he meant, I didn't have to.

"You know," he continued, "the First Amendment. Freedom of the press."

"Oh . . . yeah. Definitely," I said. Well, I *could* have done it for that reason—maybe on a subconscious level.

"Even though we're only in high school, we have rights, too. If we told who we saw, the next thing they'd want us to do was reveal our sources. No good journalist does that." Daniel stopped and turned to me. "And there was another reason I couldn't reveal my source."

I really hoped it was some shallow reason like mine so I wouldn't have to feel like such a sleaze. So far Daniel seemed more concerned about the Constitution, while I was more worried about my crush.

"What was the reason?" I said.

Daniel leaned toward me and I got a whiff of a woodsy smell. "You promise you won't tell?"

I shook my head.

"You know my sister's a cheerleader. Well, she's dating Austin Morell, one of the guys on the team. She's got kind of a big mouth, and when we were talking about school, it slipped out that the players were planning something at Saint Bart's."

Okay. Daniel lied because of loyalty.

I lied because of lust.

Could I feel any guiltier?

"It wouldn't have been fair to get her in trouble just because she can't keep a secret," Daniel added.

"Uh, sure, no," I said. "Definitely not."

He looked at his watch. "The bell's about to ring. I guess we may as well go on to second period."

"Guess so." As Daniel and I headed toward the stairwell, I thought of one more thing. "Would you have told if those guys had been doing something really wrong?" I said.

"Like what?"

"Like if they'd succeeded in cutting down the tree."

Daniel shrugged. "I don't know."

"What if they'd hurt someone?"

"That's different. I definitely would have stopped it," Daniel said.

"Why?"

"I've been thinking a lot about it since last night. Maybe journalists shouldn't just report the news. When it's something you really care about, maybe you should get involved."

"Yeah, I guess so," I said. "I hadn't really thought about it."

"See you seventh period," Daniel said. He climbed the stairs two at a time and I headed toward my U.S. History classroom.

Had Daniel Cummings and I just had a meaningful conversation?

Amazing what could happen when you shared a pair of handcuffs with someone.

EIGHT

Emily Back on Course

"I am sooo sorry," I told Lindsay, raising my voice to be heard over the commotion in the cafeteria.

She swallowed a mouthful of peanut butter and jelly sandwich. "It's okay. I was just worried about you. I didn't know if I'd see you today. Or if you'd still be in jail or something."

"I think it's pretty safe to say I won't be going to the big house," I said.

"Good to hear," Lindsay said, adding, "you know your car's still at my house. I told my mom you were sick so I drove you home."

"Yeah, my dad dropped me off this morning. It was a good opportunity for him to yell at me some more."

"You can ride home with me and pick it up," Lindsay said.

"Thanks." I was just about to tell Lindsay about the weirdness in the principal's office when Brian sat on the bench next to me.

"Hey," I said. My stomach flipped like a cheerleader and my pulse raced. Was it possible to have the same bodily responses to being approached by cops *and* your crush? That just seemed wrong.

Brian leaned closer. "Can I talk to you for a minute?"

I turned to Lindsay, who raised her eyebrows and stifled a grin.

"Be back in a sec," I said, following Brian, who was now heading out into the hall.

He looked to see if anyone was around and came a little closer.

Brain to knees: Please stay locked in place.

"Hey," he said. "I just wanted to thank you for keeping everything that happened on the DL."

Oh my God. He knew I'd followed him.

"I heard that you and Daniel saw the whole thing at Saint Bart's and didn't tell who was there."

I felt myself frowning and tried to stop. Not a good look. "Who told you?"

Brian put his backpack on the floor and leaned against the wall. "Austin. He's going out with Brianna Cummings."

Man, did that girl *ever* keep her mouth shut?

"I know you and Daniel were doing something for the school paper when you saw us. She said you guys didn't turn us in because of the First Amendment or something."

I smiled. "Freedom of the press and all." Yes, that was why our forefathers had fought so hard. So that I, Emily Bennet, would have the freedom to press my lips against Brian Harrington's.

Brian nodded. "Anyway, I just wanted to say thanks and to invite you to Austin's party. Oh, and you can bring Daniel."

Did he think Daniel and I were a couple? "Um, thanks," I said, "but, you know, Daniel and I are just, um, reporters together. We're not even friends."

Was that a little smile on Brian's face? Did it matter to him that Daniel and I weren't going out?

"That's cool," he said. "Then you can bring your friend, uh—what's her name, with the nervous fingers."

"She's a piano player," I said, realizing I had probably just uttered the all-time stupidest response to a party invitation ever. I could feel the moisture leaving my mouth and finding its way to the palms of my hands. "But, thanks for the invite," I mumbled through desert-dry lips. "We'll be there."

Just then Brian's posse burst through the cafeteria doors, saving me from Stupid Response No. 2. "Guess I better go," he said, slinging his backpack on one shoulder. He took a couple of steps and turned back around. "One more thing," he said. "Grams has that letter for you to give to the boat captain."

He got in step with his group and yelled back to me. "My parents won't be home, but don't worry, the maid will let you in."

Great. I headed back to Lindsay and my lunch.

"What was that all about?" Lindsay said.

"Kind of a good news/bad news thing. The good news being that we're both invited to Austin's party. The bad news being that Grams is expecting me to pick up a note for Captain Miguel tonight and Brian won't be there."

Lindsay wrinkled her nose. "I'm invited to a party at Austin's. How'd that happen?"

"I'll explain later," I said. "Right now I'm more concerned about the bad news. Want to meet Grams tonight?"

Lindsay practically choked on her granola bar. "No way. Not after last night. You're on your own."

I crinkled my lunch bag and tossed it into a nearby wastebasket. Things were definitely not going the way I'd planned.

Seventh period was Advanced Journalism II, which meant all the students in the class were staff writers for the *Crestview Courier*. It also meant we were all vying for front page articles that could reap awards and scholarships. So when Ms. Keenan assigned Daniel and me to cowrite a story about the upcoming junior prom, we both let out a simultaneous sigh of disappointment. You don't win contests by writing about tuxedos and taffeta.

Daniel picked up the desk in front of me, turned it around, and sat facing me. "So how do you want to do this?"

I opened my notebook. "I guess we could do some interviews—find out what people have planned."

Daniel faked a yawn.

Now *that* was the Daniel I knew and loathed. Arrogant. Obnoxious. "Excuse me," I said. "Have you got a better idea?"

"Not yet," Daniel said. "But I think I can come up with something more original than that. Think outside the box. I bet you were one of those little kids who traced every picture when you colored and then stayed perfectly inside the lines."

He was right, but I didn't want to admit it. "We don't have that much time," I said. "Ms. Keenan wants the story by next week. We have to think of an angle, research it, and write it by then. Some of us have a life."

"You know," Daniel said, "people spend obscene amounts of money on proms; we can do an exposé on the gross materialism of a decaying ritual. Or—" Daniel moved to a chair in front of a computer, hit a few keys, and clicked the mouse. I couldn't see exactly what he was doing until he called me over.

I dragged a chair next to him and rolled my eyes. He'd found a picture of a sexy prom dress online. He'd photoshopped it, and at the top, he'd written, "Feeling *Prom*iscuous?"

I glared at him. "Are you going to take this seriously or not?"

He gave a fake pout. "What?" he said. "Sex sells."

"So do eggs. Shall we call it, 'Feeling Like a *Prom*elet?'"

"Go ahead and laugh. But if we don't do something original here, neither of us stands a chance at getting editor next year."

It was the first time we'd ever verbalized the fact that we both wanted the same job. I lowered my eyes almost involuntarily.

"It's okay," he said. "Competition isn't just for jocks. A little healthy intellectual competition is a good thing."

I looked at the clock. Seventh period was nearly over and Lindsay would be waiting to take me back to my car. I stuck my notebook in my backpack and slung it over my shoulder. "You're right," I said with a nod. "I want editor. So any ideas on how to work around this stupid assignment?"

"Why don't we each work on an idea and see who comes up with the best one. You've got a week. Deal?" He extended his hand.

I didn't like taking orders from Daniel, but I really wanted to get out of the room and meet Lindsay. I shook his hand reluctantly. "Deal."

NINE

Emily Delivers Once Again

For a second time, I found myself in a starring role on Harringtoncam. But instead of a shirtless Brian, a smiling woman named Evelyn greeted me.

"Come in," she said in a Jamaican accent. "Miss Lily is expectin' you."

I followed her through the house and toward the back. The aroma of curry met me as she opened the cottage door. Lily was at the stove with her back to us. She turned and smiled like a kid getting into the chocolate stash.

"Miss Lily, what am I gonna do with you?" The woman shook her head. "You know that's my job."

"Oh, go shuffle your ball change." Lily grinned, then

turned to me. "I heard that in an old movie with Elizabeth Taylor."

I nodded and caught a whiff of the sweet and spicy smell of mingling flavors on the stove.

Lily raised the spoon to her mouth. "Perfect." She set it in a spoon-shaped dish beside the stove that read GRANDMA. My heart swelled like the bubbling curry. What a sweet guy Brian was, buying such a cute gift for his Grams! So what if he tried to cut down an old tree? I had to give him points for being a good grandson.

Lily ladled a spoonful of the mixture onto one of the two plates on the table and handed it to me. Onions, carrots, and chunks of chicken in brown gravy spread out on the shiny white plate ringed with daisies. It was a sight worthy of one of my mother's photographs. Lily fixed another dish and handed it to Evelyn. "Try it," she demanded.

"Now, Miss Lily, you know I'm supposed to be doin' the cookin' tonight. I never would have given you my recipe if I thought you were goin' to take my job away."

Lily ignored Evelyn and stood over us until we picked up our forks and dug in.

"Mmmm." It was delicious at first, but then suddenly the back of my throat began to burn. I reached for the glass of water on the table and chugged half of it.

"Not used to a little spice in your life, heh?" Lily said with a chuckle.

I shook my head and took another gulp.

"Well, maybe we can fix that," Lily said.

"It's okay, I'm really not hungry."

Lily laughed. "Oh, I wasn't talking about that kind of spice. I saw the way you were looking at my grandson last night."

My face felt as hot as the curry. Did this woman ever edit what came out of her mouth?

Before I could answer, she continued, "You know you're just the kind of girl he needs. Not that Clausen girl with the skimpy clothes and the pierced belly button."

Hmm. Maybe Lily was more sane than I'd given her credit for.

She winked. "Next time I see Brian, I'll put in a good word for you."

I smiled. Winking language now translated.

Awesome.

Evelyn tried to force Lily to sit at the table and use the second plate, but she insisted on standing at the stove and eating out of the pot. "I might just have to buy another place setting," Lily said, looking at me.

"And maybe a fourth settin', too," Evelyn said in her singsong way.

"Oh, you," Lily shot back playfully. "You've been reading too many of those romance novels of yours. Captain Miguel is just a fan of my dancing."

Evelyn laughed. "If any man wrote me a note like that, I'd be jumpin' his bones."

This was definitely not a picture I wanted to conjure in my mind. But, suddenly, I wished I'd read that note.

"It was such a lovely sentiment, wasn't it?" Lily said, with a dreamy look in her eyes.

For a second I felt like I was in a movie on Lifetime about second chances for older women. "What did the note say?"

Lily put down the spoon and looked toward the ceiling. "He told me my dancing made the world a more beautiful place."

It wasn't exactly the stuff of romance novels, but I guessed if I were Lily, it would come close. She was probably way over the heaving-bosom stage in her life. And being told you made the world more beautiful was a pretty big compliment.

It reminded me of a book my mother used to read to me when I was little—*Miss Rumphius*—about an old woman who throws seeds everywhere and eventually beautiful flowers grow all over the countryside. In the story, Miss Rumphius tells her niece that she should do something to make the world more beautiful, too. I remembered asking my mother what *she* wanted to do to make the world more beautiful.

"Take pictures of mountains and oceans," she'd said. Mom was a nature lover at heart.

Wow. How had she gotten from that to taking pictures of poultry painted with antiseptic ointment?

I used to try to think of something I could do to make the world more beautiful. But I hadn't thought about it for a long time.

Lily opened a wooden box and pulled out a small envelope. "I guess I shouldn't forget to give you this." She placed the note firmly into the palm of my hand. "Will you see that the captain gets it?"

"Sure," I said, taking the envelope, which gave off a faint whiff of curry and cologne. "White Shoulders?" I said, recognizing the smell from my grandmother's bedroom.

"You've got a good nose," Lily said, adding, "it's not what I'd choose, but Brian's heart was in the right place."

That's for sure. His heart, his abs, his pecs, all his parts in the right place. Unfortunately, I couldn't wait around for those parts to appear. I had homework to do.

I stuck the note in my pocket and thanked Lily and Evelyn for the food, or "cuisine" as they called it.

"I'll be waiting for the captain's response," Lily called out as Evelyn led me across the patio toward the main house.

Another response? I hadn't thought this out very well. If the captain had another note, then surely Lily would have another one, and then the captain would have another one, and then . . . I could be doing this gig till I left for college!

Messenger girl for the aged was not what I signed up for. I was supposed to deliver a note, get Brian to notice me, and then live happily ever after with Brian and his abs. Instead I seemed destined to live happily ever after with the early bird dinner crowd.

The second I stepped on my porch, Brian's car pulled into his driveway. We'd just missed each other. I thought about going back, but I wasn't sure what I'd say. So far, the only thing we had in common was an attempted matchmaking and an attempted misdemeanor. Not the beginnings of a great relationship. At least not yet. Then suddenly I realized we did have something to talk about—Austin's party.

I ran across the yard, nearly tripping over a sprinkler head. "Hey, Brian," I yelled, just as he put his key in the front door lock.

"Hey," he said, turning around. Was that a smile on his face? Was he happy to see me?

"How's it going?" I asked.

"Doin' well," he said. "Did you see Grams yet?"

"Yeah. I just wanted to know about Austin's party. When is it?" How lame! Talk about overanxious. "Lindsay wanted to know," I added quickly. "I think she's got a piano thing or something coming up."

Brian took his key out of the lock and dropped his

gym bag on the porch. A good sign he wasn't rushing to get away from me. "Good thing you asked," he said. "Austin changed it to this Friday night. His parents are going away for the weekend."

"Cool," I said. I wondered if he would have remembered to tell me if I hadn't asked. "What time?" I added.

"About nine. And, just so you know, it's a *G* party."

"A *G* party?"

"Yeah. Everyone's supposed to dress in something that begins with the letter *G*."

I must have had a puzzled look on my face because Brian started laughing. "It was Brandy's idea."

Well, that explained it. She probably wanted to go as a G-string. "So what are you wearing?" I asked.

"I haven't thought about it yet. Any ideas?"

I paused. "A ghost?" I blurted. Talk about uncreative.

Brian laughed again. Sigh. I really loved the way the dimple below his right eye crinkled when he did that. "Actually, I thought of that one."

"Maybe Lily can help you come up with something."

"Maybe," Brian said, and then added, "Did she give you the note for that guy?"

I patted my pocket. "Yeah, it's right here."

"You gonna give it to him?"

"Yeah, definitely." Was there a choice here that I was missing? "Why do you ask?"

Brian shrugged. "My parents are a little freaked out

that Grams might get into some weird relationship."

"It didn't seem like the captain was crazy or anything. Just that he liked her dancing."

"I'm sure you're right." Brian paused. "How're you going to find him again?"

"I guess I'll go back to the *Conga Queen*."

"By yourself?"

Okay, Emily, slow down. "Um, I hadn't really thought about it . . . You want to come, too? I mean to check out the captain again?"

"Sure," he said. "When do you want to go?"

I knew that the *Conga Queen* sailed on weekends at noon. "We could probably catch him before the boat goes out on Saturday—maybe about eleven thirty."

He shook his head. "I've got practice all day and the game against Saint Bart's at night. Can we make it another day?"

The mere mention of Saint Bart's made me even more nervous, but I didn't want to lose this opportunity. "Sure," I said. "Sunday?"

Brian picked up his gym bag. "As long as it's in the morning."

"That's fine," I said. "Meet you here at eleven."

He nodded.

Maybe this matchmaking thing had potential after all.

TEN

Emily Full of Hot Air?

I was lying on my bed that evening, replaying the whole scene between Brian and me, when the phone rang.

"Hey, Emily."

A guy's voice. My stomach fluttered for a second, but then I realized it was too deep to be Brian's.

"It's Daniel."

"Oh. Hi." Jeez. You get hauled to jail with someone once and suddenly he's your close friend, calling you during the most crucial part of your best daydream ever.

He cleared his throat. "My dad wanted me to call you to figure out a time to start working on our community service project."

Somehow I must have been sleeping through a chapter of my life. "We have a community service project *together*?"

"Uh, yeah," Daniel said. "Remember last night? The handcuffs. The cops."

I sat straight up in bed. That was one Sunday memory I was hoping to replace soon.

"When my dad was talking to the cops, he told them he'd see that we did community service."

"You mean, you and me, together?" I knew I'd agreed to community service, but *with* Daniel?

"Yeah, apparently your parents were all for it, too."

My parents probably would have agreed to anything to get me out of the police station that night. "Do we have to do it now? I mean, can't we put it off for a while?"

"I don't know," Daniel said. "My dad says he wants us to get started."

Daniel's father was an intimidating guy. And Daniel wasn't likely to be less annoying in the future, so I gave in. "What do you want to do?" I walked to my window and watched the light go on in Brian's room.

"I was thinking—there's a nursing home not too far from Crestview. You want to go there after school on Friday?"

I tried to pay attention to Daniel, but Brian's silhouette was way more interesting. I watched his shadowy outline go from the closet to his computer. "Um, yeah, sounds great," I said mechanically.

"Okay, then, you want to meet in the school parking lot?"

Suddenly Daniel's words registered. "Did you say Friday?" I said. "That's no good."

Daniel paused. "You just said it sounded great." He sounded irritated.

"Well, yeah," I said, trying to make it seem like he'd misunderstood me. "Friday's are good, but not this Friday. I'm going to a party that night. I need time to get ready."

"I almost forgot—Austin's."

"Oh," I said, trying to hide my disappointment that Daniel had been invited, too. I'd thought it was kind of an exclusive thing. "You're going?"

"Yeah, you know it's the whole cheerleader-slash-sister connection. How'd you get invited?"

Was that an insult? Was Daniel implying that I was out of my league?

"I didn't mean that how it sounded," Daniel said, before I could respond.

"Oh, really?"

"No, I mean, yes. I just meant there's usually a certain crowd that goes to those parties—the same people all the time. I've never seen you there before."

I guess I could forgive him. "Well, there's nothing

like almost being arrested to bump you up the status stepladder."

Daniel laughed. "Crazy how it works, huh? So what are you going as?"

"I hadn't really thought about it yet," I said. "How about you?"

Without a pause, Daniel answered, "A Goober."

"A what?"

"You know those chocolate-covered peanuts you eat at the movie theater."

Leave it to a guy who buys his clothes at the thrift store to come up with an outrageous idea like that. "How're you going to find a Goober costume?" Even the thrift stores wouldn't have something like that.

"I'm making it," he said, "out of a big brown garbage bag. I already cut a hole in the bottom for my head to go through. Before the party, I'll stuff it with newspaper and pull the ties around my legs. I can make one for you, too."

"I think I'll stick to something more conventional." I was pretty sure a Goober costume was not going to show off my best assets to Brian.

"Suit yourself," Daniel said. Then added with a chuckle, "literally."

"Please," I said. "If you come up with any ideas that don't involve me going as a huge brown ball, let me know."

"Hmm, I'll have to think about it. In the meantime, what about Saturday for the nursing home?"

"That's fine," I answered, but my mind was already miles away, trying to come up with a costume that would be clever, cute, and not mistaken for the daily trash.

My eyes crossed as I watched the green balloon grow bigger before my eyes.

"Too big, too big," Lindsay yelled. "It's ready to pop."

I pulled the balloon from my lips, let a little bit of air out, and knotted the end. "How many of these things do you think I'll need?"

Lindsay looked down at the small pile of balloons bouncing between the two beds in my room. "Stand up and let me take a look at you," she said.

I twirled around like a runway model.

"In my professional opinion," Lindsay said, "about ten more."

I picked up another balloon. "And which profession would that be?" I asked before taking a deep breath.

"Grape expert," Lindsay said. She balanced a balloon in the palm of her hand and gently slapped it in the air several times. "Tell me again how you're going to wear these to the party tomorrow night?"

I tried to remember what I'd originally envisioned when I decided it was a good idea to go as grapes. "I'm not sure. I just know I have to attach them to something so I can put them on at the last minute—or else I won't be able to sit in the car."

"Yeah," Lindsay said. "We'll have to do a last-minute thing in the parking lot for me, too. You've got to wrap me in aluminum foil."

I laughed. "That did *not* sound right. Please promise me you will never ever say that in public."

Lindsay held up her right hand. "Promise. But you have to promise me that you won't leave me alone at the party."

Lindsay hadn't been too thrilled about going to Austin's. The athletes and cheerleaders weren't exactly our crowd. But after I talked her into it, she got excited about the costume. She'd decided to go as a stick of gum. She planned to wear a pink turtleneck that would peek out of the aluminum foil wrapping. We both thought we were pretty clever.

Lindsay blew up a few more balloons as I looked through my closet for something to attach them to. I finally found an old green T-shirt and held it up for Lindsay to inspect. "What if we pin the balloons to this shirt and then I'll put it on at the last minute?"

Lindsay shrugged. "Works for me. But what about the bottom? Do you have any green pants?"

"How about brown? My legs can be like the stem of the grapes."

"Perfect," Lindsay said. "Now can we eat?"

I'd lured Lindsay over my house to blow up balloons with the promise of pizza for dinner. I'd overheard my mom on the phone ordering some. I could smell the crust and the cheese as we walked down the hall to the kitchen.

But when we got there, I stopped short. "Eww, what have you done with our dinner?"

"Sorry," my mom said. "I had to do it—to paraphrase an old joke, 'It is better to look good than to taste good.' I'm doing a photo shoot for a flyer."

"Right," I said, staring at the pizzas. They were spread out on different levels on the kitchen table, but had been pretty much rendered inedible. By the looks of the bottles and containers on the counter, I figured out my mom had doused the toppings with oil so they wouldn't look dried out and painted the crust a more golden brown with shoe polish.

Lindsay looked at me with pleading eyes.

"Um, Mom, could you give us some money for pizza that doesn't look as good but tastes okay?" I said.

She dug a twenty out of a kitchen drawer and handed it to me. "Bring the leftovers home."

As we backed out of the driveway, I caught a glimpse of Brian shooting baskets out front. I beeped the horn and waved.

"Aren't we chummy these days?" Lindsay said.

"What's going on with you two, anyway?"

I shrugged. "I'm not sure. He's either grateful that I saved the team's butt by not saying who was at Saint Bart's, happy that I'm being nice to his grandmother, or—and this is the one I'm hoping for—finally aware of my existence as a potential girlfriend."

"Maybe a little of all three," Lindsay said.

I turned onto the highway. "Maybe I'll find out tomorrow night at the party."

ELEVEN

Emily Reaches Shoreline

I shivered in the ocean breeze. I was wearing the tank top I'd planned to wear under my costume, but I had to help Lindsay before I put my balloon shirt on. I was wrapping her like a mummy in aluminum foil, when a few other cars pulled into the parking lot of Austin's condo building.

"Ohhhh, sexy!" a voice yelled toward us. It belonged to Randy Clausen, who was dressed as a Girl Scout, complete with a box of Thin Mint cookies in her hand. I was pretty sure it was her actual Girl Scout uniform from fourth grade. She could barely button the shirt, and the skirt just covered her butt. She looked like a middle-aged perv's fantasy girl.

The guy with her, who was dressed in huge pants, a couple of T-shirts, and lots of gold chains, put his arm around her. "We're the gangsta and the Girl Scout," he announced.

"I'm a stick of gum," Lindsay blurted. Her voice cracked.

The gangsta smirked as he passed by. "Hope nobody chews you up and spits you out."

"That was rude," Lindsay said, holding her leg out for me to wrap.

"They're not exactly the most sensitive crowd," I said. "But really, Brian is nothing like them. You should see him with his grandmother."

"Whatever," Lindsay said. "You just better stick by me tonight. Ha. Get it. Stick by me. I'm gum."

I stared at Lindsay, shining under the glow of the parking lot lights. "Please don't say that inside." I couldn't decide if she looked like a stick of gum or someone's Thanksgiving leftovers, but I decided to keep my mouth shut. I had my own problems trying to get my T-shirt on without popping any of the balloons.

The lobby of Austin's building looked like a ballroom. Everyone was waiting for the one elevator that went to the penthouse. Lindsay and I stood farthest from the crowd, next to a huge flower arrangement in a vase the size of our bathtub.

I scanned the lobby. Not as many ghosts and

goalkeepers as I'd expected. Someone in a gorilla suit stood in front of the elevator making grunting noises. A couple of people wore what looked like their older siblings' Crestview graduation caps and gowns. Ariana James, the tallest and thinnest of the cheerleaders, was all decked out as a geisha, which seemed extremely appropriate given her reputation.

I wondered if coming had been a big mistake. A lot of these people weren't in the classes that Lindsay and I took. Sure, they were wearing costumes, but even the ones whose faces were in full view looked unfamiliar. That is, until Daniel burst through the door in his garbage bag. "It's Goober t-i-i-ime!" he yelled. Then he pulled out a large box and began distributing Goobers to the group. I had to admit, he knew how to work a crowd. Everyone was cheering and holding out their hands for candy.

When he got near Lindsay and me, he stopped, looked us over, and nodded. "Very creative."

Behind him, his sister, Brianna, shivered in her genie costume, a bare midriff top with sheer sleeves that matched her puffy pants. Daniel stepped aside so she could join us. "She'll grant you three wishes," he said.

Brianna smiled as if she'd heard the joke a few too many times already. "Austin's waiting for me," she said. "I'm moving closer to the elevator."

As the crowd slowly moved forward, Lindsay, Daniel, and I finally got close enough to get on with the next group. But once everyone squished in, there was no room for me and my balloons. I stood before the open doors, staring at Lindsay, Daniel, two ghosts, three goalkeepers, and Goofy.

"Sorry, no room for the grapes," one of the ghosts said. Then he quickly added, "Don't *whine* about it."

As the elevator doors closed, the mocking laughter oozed through the crack and I stood alone in the lobby.

After a few minutes, a golfer and a grumpy old man appeared. Then, suddenly, I spotted something shiny coming toward me. As it got closer, I recognized a breastplate, a sword, and . . . Brian's face. My heart swelled like one of my balloons. Then quickly deflated when I saw who was behind him.

Brandy Clausen. All decked out in a gymnastics outfit that I'm pretty sure would have been banned after one trick on the balance beam.

Hadn't Brian told Grams that Brandy wasn't his girlfriend? Why were they together?

"Hey," Brian said, "cool. Grapes." He spun around. "Can you guess who I am? Grams gave me the idea."

I thought for a minute. "You're Galahad, right?"

Then, as if on cue, Brandy rubbed her practically naked gymnast body up against him and purred, "My knight in shining armor."

I looked down at my costume. Why oh why hadn't I thought to come as Guinevere?

When the elevator doors opened, we all stepped in. At least I fit in this time.

I punched the PH button and wondered what to expect when I got upstairs. I'd never been to a popular crowd party before. Most of the parties Lindsay and I went to were pretty tame. Pizza, popcorn, a movie. Twice a year—at Christmas and at the end of the school year—a few of us would get together and Lindsay's mother would let us eat the food gifts she'd gotten from her fourth graders while we sorted through her other presents to see if there was anything we wanted.

The minute the elevator doors slid open onto a makeshift dance floor with blaring music, it was pretty clear this party would be nothing like sharing cheese logs and sifting through a stack of Best-Teacher-in-the-World mugs.

While several couples were grinding in the middle of the living room, others hovered around a bar in the corner of the room. Behind it, Austin stood surrounded by several liquor bottles and various mugs and glasses with sports team logos.

"There you are," Lindsay said. She grabbed my hand and pulled me toward her. At the same time, Brandy tugged on Brian's sword and dragged him in the direction of the bar. Brian rolled his eyes and mouthed "help" toward me.

Help? Me? Brian wanted *me* to help him get away from Brandy Clausen? Hooray! It was like a dream come true. I was trying to figure out exactly how to do that when Lindsay whispered, "What do we do now?"

I knew what *I* wanted to do—rescue Brian from the Clausen clutches. But I couldn't abandon Lindsay. "Try to mingle?" I said.

Lindsay nodded as we stood there awkwardly, looking around for a way to blend in. I imagined how dorky we probably looked: a stick of gum and a bunch of grapes amid a sea of half-clothed gymnasts, Girl Scouts, and geishas rubbing up against one another on the dance floor.

Suddenly, I heard a familiar rattling noise behind me. I turned to find Daniel shaking his Goobers box over his head in time to the music. "So what do you think?" he said.

"About what?" I yelled over the music.

"You know, the whole half-naked girls-slash-athletes party scene. It's the American Dream, isn't it?"

Again, *that* was the kind of superior attitude that annoyed me about Daniel. Why couldn't he just enjoy the party? Why did he have to analyze everything to death? This wasn't psychology class.

"Why do you come if you have such contempt for it?" I said.

Before Daniel could answer, Lindsay broke in, "What are they doing over there with the lemons?" She scrunched her nose as we watched Brianna suck on a slice and swig something out of a tiny Miami Heat glass.

"Chocolate cake shots," Daniel said. "It's some kind of liqueur with vodka and sugar on the lemon. Austin's got this party thing down to a science. Beer doesn't get the girls drunk enough because they don't like the taste, and they don't want to gain weight. The shots taste good and get them drunk faster."

"What's so great about that?" Lindsay said.

Daniel laughed. "Think about it."

Lindsay's aluminum foil sounded a nervous crinkle.

I glared back at Daniel. "You seem to know a lot about these parties. Again, I ask, why do you come if you hate it so much?"

Daniel popped a Goober into his mouth and held out the box toward me. I shook my head. "I don't hate it," he said. "I don't love it either. As for the reason I come—" He gestured toward the bar with his head. "She's over there, chugging a chocolate cake shot."

I followed his signal but there were about four girls in the vicinity. Then I noticed Ariana's blond hair streaming down her bare, geisha back. Of course, even an outsider like Daniel would be in love with a goddess. I was a little disappointed. I thought he'd go for a brainier girl rather than a Barbie replica.

"Isn't she dating Garrett?" The team's best center was a male version of Ariana, tall and gorgeous.

"What?" Daniel said. He almost dropped his Goobers. "I'm not talking about Ariana. I'm talking about my sister."

"Your sister?"

"Yeah, I may not be able to stop her from getting drunk, but I can make sure she doesn't do anything stupid while she *is* drunk. She's only fifteen. According to studies her brain isn't developed enough to make good decisions."

"And yours is?" The question popped out of my mouth without thinking. I hadn't meant to insult Daniel, but he was only seventeen and, after all, he *was* standing there in a garbage bag stuffed with newspaper. How mature could his brain be?

"Look who's talking," he shot back. "I'm not the only ex-con in the room."

Lindsay leaned toward us and whispered. "Technically, you're not ex-cons. You weren't convicted of anything."

Daniel laughed. "I know. I was just having fun with Miss Maturity here."

Just as I was trying to think of a good comeback, I felt my grapes jostle. A crowd blew past us and down a hallway.

"Where are they all going?" Lindsay said.

"Chill room," Daniel said. "You want to see it? It's really the media room—wide-screen TV, state-of-the-art stereo and speakers."

As we started toward the room, I caught a glimpse of Brian, who was finally away from Brandy. Now was my chance to go talk to him. "I'll be there in a second," I told Lindsay. "I just want to get a drink."

She glared at me. "Diet Coke," I assured her. "You guys want one?"

They shook their heads.

I maneuvered my way into a spot between Ariana and Brian, whose back was toward me. I tapped him on the shoulder. "Do you know where the Diet Coke is?"

He spun around. "Hey, Emily, I was wondering where you were."

Be still my balloons. "Really?"

"Yeah. How do you like the party?"

"Pretty good so far."

"Here," he said, handing me a glass. "I'll get the soda."

I was sure I wore a stupid grin on my face as I watched him walk toward the kitchen. That is, until a certain Girl Scout took a toothpick off the bar and stuck it into one of my balloons. The warm glow I was feeling was suddenly interrupted by a *pop, pop, popping* against my back.

"Hey, grape juice!" Austin yelled, as Randy and her gangsta boyfriend stuck me again. I suddenly understood the attraction of getting wasted. You didn't have to try all that hard to amuse yourself.

True to his Galahad alter ego, Brian appeared with the sodas, just in time to rescue me. He grabbed my elbow. "Let's get away from these guys."

We walked onto an outdoor patio that overlooked the beach to the east and downtown Fort Lauderdale to the west. "Wow!" I said.

Brian closed the doors behind us. "Pretty nice, huh? It makes the river behind our houses look like a kid's swimming pool."

"But who would Grams dance for if she lived here?" I teased.

Brian laughed. "The condominium association would probably have her arrested before she even started her dance." Then suddenly, he grabbed my shoulders and pulled me in front of him.

"What are you doing?" I cried.

"Sorry, I just spotted Brandy. I don't want her to know I'm out here."

"Oh," I said, trying to compose myself. "So I'm just a balloon barrier?"

He let go of my shoulders. "No," he said apologetically. "I mean, I do want to be away from her, but I also . . ."

Awkward silence.

"But didn't you come to the party with Brandy?" Why did I bring up *her* again?

"No," he said. "I brought her here, but I didn't come with her."

"What does that mean?"

Brian arranged his sword on his hip and sighed. "I drove her here because her father asked my father if I would. Randy had a ride with Kyle, and Brandy didn't want to go with them."

I felt like a breath I'd been holding had just been released. I hoped my relief didn't show too much as I said, "Her dad?" No matter how much I wanted a date, I'd never ask my parents to intervene.

"Yeah, my dad does business with Mr. Clausen," Brian said.

"So you aren't going out with Brandy?"

"No way," Brian said. "I don't want to sound cocky, but she wishes." Then suddenly, he grabbed my shoulders and jerked me in front of him again.

"Brandy?"

"Yeah, she just walked by," he said, adding, "so are you glad you came to the party?"

"I was until I became the entertainment at the bar."

"Forget about those idiots," he said. "I'm glad it's just us out here."

"Really?" I squeaked.

Brian smiled. "Yeah, I wanted to tell you thanks for being so nice to Grams. She doesn't get to see many people, and she just, well, seems a little happier since you came by."

"I'm here to help," I blurted. Immediately, I wanted to take the words back. What did I even mean? I tried to save myself with a question. "But why doesn't she get to see people?"

"She moved down here from New York to be with her family after my grandfather died. It was hard for her to stay alone up there with her eyesight going."

I remembered Grams squinting when she read the captain's note. "Is she going blind?"

"Oh no, not that bad," Brian said. "But she can't drive, so it's hard for her to meet people."

"Maybe Captain Miguel can change that for her," I said, smiling.

But Brian didn't seem to share my optimism. He frowned for a second and hesitated. "Uh, yeah, about that. My parents found out about the captain, and they're really upset that she wrote back to him. They don't want us to deliver the note."

"Why?" I cried. Sure it was a little gross to think of old people making out and stuff, but this was a perfect opportunity for Lily to get out and meet people.

"They're afraid she might get taken advantage of," Brian said. "She has a lot of money, and they think that makes her an easy target for crooked guys."

I laughed. "Captain Miguel doesn't exactly seem like a gigolo."

"Probably not," Brian said. "Listen, I didn't come out here to talk about my parents. Grams said something about you and it got me thinking."

I gulped. Had she told him I liked him? What about all that winking? Winking was supposed to be *in place* of coming right out and telling things. Wasn't it? "Um"—I hesitated—"what did she say?"

"She asked me how I could have let someone like you live next door for so many years and never ask you out?"

Whoa. She was good. My insides were dancing to the beat of the music behind the glass doors, but I forced myself to stay calm and respond in a cool manner. "And what did you say?"

Brian shrugged. "I said I didn't know."

Was that it? I nodded and rested my elbows on the balcony.

Brian turned and did the same.

So now what? I breathed in the salty air and shivered a little as a breeze blew by.

"You cold?" Brian said.

"A little."

He grabbed a beach towel off a chair. "Anyway . . ." Brian said, "I started thinking maybe Grams was right.

Ever since I moved here I've just hung out with Brandy, the drama queen, and her crowd. I didn't even consider that you and I could hang out. I mean—if you'd want to."

I wanted to jump up and down on the balcony and yell, "He likes me! He likes me!" Instead, I tried to keep my voice from cracking and answered, "Sure, that would be great."

"Great," he echoed, circling the beach towel tightly around my shoulders.

Suddenly I recalled the Christmas Eve that I was seven. All I'd wanted was a Fisher-Price kitchen. By accident, I'd spotted the big box in the garage, but I couldn't let on that I knew. I remembered the feeling I had that night, looking up at the tree, feeling like I'd burst with anticipation, that I'd never last till morning.

That was exactly how I felt, standing under the stars next to Brian.

TWELVE

Emily Takes Detour

Saturday morning. I opened my eyes around nine, but just lay there thinking about the night before. Had Brian Harrington actually asked me if I wanted to "hang out" with him?

I wasn't sure what that meant, but every time I thought about it, I could hardly catch my breath. I'd daydreamed about going out with Brian for so long. I closed my eyes and imagined us together at parties, at the movies, at the prom. We'd be so inseparable they'd call us "Bremily." Unfortunately, I didn't get to learn if "hanging out" and "going out" were the same for Brian.

Just when he'd tucked the towel under my chin,

Brandy burst through the French doors to the balcony and demanded that Brian drive her home. She claimed to have a migraine. Then she looked at me and made some snide remark about someone "picking my grapevine."

Brian tried to persuade her to stay, but Brandy would have none of it. "Do you want me to call my dad?" she said. "I know he'll pick me up—even though your dad told him you'd give me a ride home."

Brian looked at me and rolled his eyes. "Sorry," he said.

"It's okay," I said.

Shortly after they left, Lindsay decided she'd had enough, too. The chill room turned out to be a little too chilly. The only one who had spoken to her was Daniel. With Brian gone, I didn't have a big investment in staying, so we left.

I looked outside the window to see if Brian's car was next door. Then I remembered he said he had practice before the St. Bart's game that night. I was deep into imagining a shirtless Brian gracefully executing an overhead shot when the phone rang.

"Emily?" This time I wasn't fooled. I recognized Daniel's deep voice right away.

"What's up?" I said.

"Um, we're supposed to go to the nursing home, remember?"

“Yes,” I said, “of course I remember.” Though it *had* slipped my mind.

“I thought you might need a ride,” he said.

Even though I didn’t want to spend any more time with Daniel than I had to, I wasn’t sure where the nursing home was and I didn’t want to get lost. “I’ll meet you out front in an hour,” I said, still staring outside at Brian’s empty parking spot.

As I slid into the passenger seat, Daniel turned the radio off.

“What was that playing?” I said. “I liked it.”

“It’s a band called the Gloomy Pharmacists.”

I laughed. “I guess I’d be gloomy if I were a pharmacist.”

“Yeah,” Daniel said, “but somebody’s got to do it.”

“Why’d you turn it off?” I said.

“Habit. My dad doesn’t like us to listen to the radio when other people are in the car. He thinks it’s a good opportunity for people to *communicate* when they’re trapped in a car together.”

“Trapped, huh?”

“His word, not mine.”

An awkward silence followed as I tried to think of how Daniel and I could *communicate*. I was sure he was trying to think of something to say, too. He finally won.

“Don’t worry,” he said. “Some people get a little

freaked out when they think about nursing homes, but it's not what you think."

"How do you know what I think?"

Daniel adjusted his rearview mirror. "The amazing Daniel knows all and sees all."

"Right," I said. "I forgot about your incredible powers."

Daniel laughed.

"So what's the nursing home like if it's not what I'm thinking?"

"For starters, a lot of people there are fairly lucid. They go in and out sometimes. Some of them can carry on a pretty good conversation. Sometimes it's the same conversation over and over, but they make a lot of sense once in a while."

"How do you know so much about it?"

"I used to go there and read to a group who liked books but couldn't see well anymore. But since junior year started with all those AP classes, there's not enough time for the things I want to do." He laughed. "You know, too busy getting hauled off to jail."

"Ironic, huh? Now that's the thing bringing you back here."

Daniel shook his head. "Irony presumes that things are supposed to happen in a certain way. I don't believe that."

Now this was the intellectually smug Daniel that I

found so annoying. "What do you mean?"

"You know. Like that singer who used to be popular a while ago." Then he proceeded to screech out the lyrics, " 'Like ra-a-a-a-in on your wedding day.' "

I couldn't help but laugh. "That was really awful."

"True," Daniel said. "I never claimed I could sing. But rain on your wedding day isn't ironic at all. Who ever said there was a guarantee that it wouldn't rain on your wedding day? It's just bad luck. Maybe even bad judgment—I mean everyone knows there's a pretty good chance of rain certain months of the year. Particularly June, the most popular month for weddings."

"You're quite the romantic, aren't you?" I said.

The corner of Daniel's mouth turned up. I was beginning to recognize the look. It always came before a tease. "Not as romantic as your new friend Harrington."

My face turned red hot. I ignored the comment and pressed Daniel further on his irony theory. "What about King Midas? You know, every teacher always gives that as an example of dramatic irony."

"Could be," Daniel said, "but really . . . the guy wishes that everything he touches turns to gold. That's just bad judgment. I mean, couldn't he think ahead? Just wiping his butt would be a problem."

"Thanks for the visual," I said. "So then what you're

telling me is that it's not ironic at all that your almost arrest has brought you back to the nursing home. It was just bad judgment?"

"Could be," Daniel said. "Then again, it could have been very good judgment."

I thought I saw that curl of his lip again. I wasn't sure what he was getting at, so I changed the subject. "So what's happening with the big prom article? Got any brilliant ideas yet?"

Daniel gestured to a blue folder on the floor. "I'm glad you asked. Open it up."

The first page read only: *Prom*nivores. The second page was a list of prom expenses.

"Check it out," Daniel said. "I did a little informal survey. Last year's junior prom was called 'Some Enchanted Evening.' More like 'Some Expensive Evening.'"

Daniel really knew how to suck the magic out of things, but I had to admit he was right when I read:

Two prom tickets: average cost $140
One prom dress: average cost $175
One pair of women's shoes: average cost $85
One pair of men's shoes: average cost $90
One purse: average cost $35
One tux rental: average cost $125
One corsage: average cost $35
One boutonniere: average cost $18

Limo: average cost per couple $70
Prom pictures: average cost $25
After-prom hotel: average cost per couple $100
Total average cost: $898

"And that's only the things that are legal," Daniel said.

I closed the folder. "Wow, I can't believe men's shoes are so expensive—they're so plain."

"Is that all you have to say?" Daniel said.

I laughed. "Just kidding. Okay, you're right. It's a ridiculous expense. But what are we supposed to do about it. It's just a list—what kind of article do we write?"

Daniel pulled into the parking lot of the nursing home. "I'm not sure," he said. "I thought you could come up with that—since you don't seem to like *my* ideas."

I sneered at him and opened the car door. "I still have until Monday to come up with an idea, remember?"

Daniel closed his car door. "Fair enough."

Once we were inside the nursing home, Daniel did most of the talking to a woman at the front desk. Judging by her excitement over our presence, I guessed she hadn't been told we were there because it was police-enforced community service. A woman named Frances escorted us into a large recreation room. An institutional odor that always reminded me of chicken with rice soup met us at the door along with a tiny woman who greeted us with, "It's about time you two came to visit me." Frances brought the tiny woman to a couch and returned to explain that she greeted almost everyone that way. "She thinks you're her son and daughter-in-law," Frances whispered.

Daniel smiled. "I remember. Last year when I came, she yelled at me for not sending her flowers on Mother's Day."

I tried to get the idea of Daniel and I being a couple out my mind. "What did you say to her?" I asked.

Daniel shrugged. "I told her it wouldn't happen again."

Frances slipped her hand into the crook of Daniel's elbow. "Now, don't be modest." She turned to me. "The next day he came with a bouquet of flowers and told her it was a belated Mother's Day gift."

Daniel looked slightly embarrassed at first, and then the corner of his mouth turned up in another smirk. He looked at me and said, "Shall we mingle?"

I stayed close to him as we paused next to a table with two men playing cards. It must have been a high-stakes game because neither one of them looked up. I wasn't sure what the stakes would be in a nursing home. The green Jell-O sitting on the snack table? "What do we do?" I whispered to Daniel.

"Just talk," he said. Then he sat on a couch next to two women.

One of the women, who was wearing a flowered dress with a zipper down the front, turned to me and said, "You look just like my granddaughter."

I smiled.

"How old are you, dear?" said the other woman, who held a handkerchief in her hands.

"Sixteen," I said.

"Oh," the woman in the flowered dress said, "my granddaughter is twenty-five."

I wasn't sure whether to be happy that I appeared sophisticated enough to look like a twenty-five-year-old or depressed that I looked nine years older than I should.

"Is this your young fella?" the one with the handkerchief asked.

Then the other woman hit her lightly on the arm and scolded, "They don't call it that anymore, Esther." She turned to us. "It's Significant Other now, isn't it?"

I was just about to explain that Daniel was not my Significant Other, or any other Other for that matter, when a third woman grabbed my hand and shook it. "Nice to meet you," I said.

She looked at me with squinty eyes. "Your hands are sticky," she said. "Whadja eat?"

I pulled my hand away reflexively and then felt a little embarrassed for doing so. "Nothing," I said. Did she think I was trying to steal the green Jell-O?

The woman walked away. Daniel leaned over and whispered, "Some are more lucid than others."

After that, we talked to several people who asked us how old we were and said again and again how we reminded them of someone. After a while the woman who thought I looked like her granddaughter asked us to play the piano. "Yes, please, please," everyone began to chant.

I looked at Daniel, puzzled.

"I guess they think we know how to play."

"Do you?" I asked.

"A little. How about you?"

"Lindsay's tried to teach me a few things. You know, 'Heart and Soul' and some others."

Daniel smiled. "Well . . . let's hit it."

He grabbed my hand and brought me over to the piano where we sat next to each other on the wooden bench. Daniel looked at me and counted, "One, two, three, four." Then he promptly went into the bumpa-dumpta-bumpa-dumpta part of "Heart and Soul." After a few measures, I joined in. We played the same eight measures over and over again because neither of us knew any more.

After a while I could play it without looking down, so I watched the people around us. They all wore smiles. Some were clapping and swaying from side to side. Others tapped their feet in time with the music. And a particularly exuberant group got up to dance. I couldn't believe such a pathetic rendition of something I wasn't even sure was a song could make them so happy. I turned toward Daniel. He looked really dorky, shaking his head and lifting his hands high in the air between notes. I wasn't sure whether to laugh at him or admire him for losing himself in the music, no matter how lame it was.

After a while, Frances announced it was time for the afternoon snack. Some people came over to Daniel and me to thank us.

"So," Frances said, "will you come again?"

Daniel looked at me as if he were waiting for an answer. "Um, sure," I said. I didn't know exactly how many times Daniel had told his father we would go to the nursing home, and I didn't want to be the one to say no in front of Frances. She seemed so nice.

"Hungry?" Daniel asked, once we were back in the car.

I *was* hungry, but did I want to spend a whole meal with Mr. Arrogance? Hunger won out and I ended up at Char-Hut, sitting across from Daniel, watching him eat a very messy veggie burger.

"It's good," he said. "You should try it."

I stabbed a piece of chicken in my salad. "No, thanks," I said. "Veggie burgers are one of those things that even my mother couldn't make look appealing. They just look like orange burgers. Yuck."

Daniel took a huge bite of the sandwich and licked some ketchup off his lower lip. "Sometimes looks can be deceiving."

THIRTEEN

Emily Breezes Through

Brian curved around the causeway onto A1A. The view to my right turned from concrete and glass to golden sunlight sparkling on the water. I tried to capture and freeze the whole picture of me sitting in Brian Harrington's car with the gorgeous backdrop of Fort Lauderdale beach.

We drove through a gate into a parking lot next to several boats. "I hope this isn't a mistake," Brian shouted above the car radio. "I had to lie to my parents about where I was going."

"I'm sure it'll be okay," I yelled back.

As I stepped out of the car, the gravel crunched under my feet. "I think it's over there," I said, pointing toward a couple of large boats with open seating on top. The wind blew my hair into my face and I stumbled on some stones.

Brian put his arm around my waist. "You okay?"

"It's just the rocks," I said, stumbling again. Or maybe the fact that Brian Harrington's bicep was draped across my back. This is it, I thought. This is what it feels like to be so close to Brian that it's actually *normal* for him to be touching me. I wanted to fold myself into the crook of his arm and stay there forever. But I kept on walking.

When we got to the *Conga Queen*, Captain Miguel was nowhere in sight. I turned to Brian. "I guess we just wait for him on the dock here."

We sat, dangling our feet and watching the fish swim beneath us. My stomach fluttered like the fish tails as Brian's leg brushed against mine.

After a few minutes of silence, Brian and I began to talk at the same time. "You go," he said.

"Oh, I was just going to ask about the game—against St. Bart's."

Brian's face brightened. "Didn't you hear? We won!"

"Wow," I said. "Great." It was hard to ignore basketball news at Crestview, but I'd managed to maintain my ignorance of it—until now.

Brian laughed and revealed that hidden dimple below his eye. "So, you're not exactly a basketball fan."

I spotted a tiny fish scurrying to catch up with the rest of the school. "Who at Crestview isn't a basketball fan?" I hoped that was vague enough.

Brian plucked a pebble from behind us and threw it toward a loop in a nearby rope. "Yes!" he shouted, when it went through the circle and plunked into the water. "Next weekend we go to state."

"Cool," I said.

Brian reached for another rock and then spotted the captain coming down the dock. "Is that the guy?" he said.

"That's him." I stood and straightened out my jeans and tank top.

Captain Miguel approached us and tilted his hat. "Good afternoon. May I help you?"

I chuckled inside at his formality. Lily would love that. "I don't know if you remember me, but . . ."

"Lily's neighbor!" he exclaimed. "Ah. Of course. I have been hoping to see you again. You gave her my note?"

"Yes." I gestured toward Brian, who was now standing. "And this is Lily's grandson, Brian."

Captain Miguel grabbed Brian's hand and shook it for several seconds. "Your grandmother is a wonderful woman. She spreads much happiness by her dancing."

Brian nodded awkwardly.

"So what brings you back to the *Conga Queen*?" the

captain said. "You want to take another cruise—so soon?"

"Oh, no," I said, unzipping my purse and riffling through the junk until I found the note. "This is from Lily," I said, handing it to him.

His sunburned face flushed as I placed the sealed envelope in his hands. He accepted it with reverence and said, "Wait, please. Right here." Then he disappeared onto the *Conga Queen*. About a minute or so later, he returned with another note, again in the shape of a boat. Wow. He must have taken a speed-writing course.

He handed it to me. "I have been saving this. For your return. You will give it to Lily?"

I shrugged, not knowing what to answer in front of Brian. I knew his family wasn't thrilled by the whole matchmaking thing, but I couldn't tell Captain Miguel that the Harringtons saw him as the star in their version of *Deuce Bigalow: Hispanic Gigolo*. "Sure," I said.

The captain looked at his watch. "I must go now to get my passengers." He smiled, shook our hands, and then walked toward a crowd waiting to get on the *Conga Queen*.

I looked at Brian uneasily. "Um. He's a cool guy, isn't he?"

"Seems like it," Brian said. "It's just weird. You know. That someone would be interested in Grams, like . . . that way."

I didn't ask what he meant by "that way." I definitely did *not* want to think about Grams and Captain Miguel doing it on the high seas.

We got back into the convertible. I slid the captain's note into my purse and inhaled the sea air.

"What will you do with the note?" Brian said.

I knew how Brian's family felt about Grams and the captain, but I didn't think he felt the same way. "I don't know. Bring it over to your grandmother later?" I paused. "Or else you can give it to her."

"Oh, no," Brian said. "My mom'll kill me if I get more involved in this."

"But don't you think Grams will be disappointed if the captain doesn't respond?"

Brian frowned. "I guess you're right. Maybe you can bring it over tonight. I'll be home alone with Grams."

Hmm. Was he trying to tell me something? Was this the beginning of us "hanging out"?

"My parents are going out to dinner with Mr. and Mrs. Clausen," he added.

Suddenly, a picture of Brandy Clausen's face wormed its way into my consciousness. I was silent for a minute, and then finally got enough courage up to ask, "How was Brandy when you dropped her off at home Friday night?" If he did indeed drop her off.

"She was fine, as usual. She's been pulling this ever since we sort of dated last year. Her migraines always seem to come when everyone else is having a good time."

"So, um, what did you do then?"

"I took her home, but only after I had to hear all about the weekend spa camp she and Randy are going to before prom."

"Spa camp?"

Brian laughed. "Yeah, I tuned out for most of it, but I think you just go there and get facials and massages and stuff."

"Hmm." I said. "Maybe she and Randy the Girl Scout will earn their massage badges."

Brian laughed again. "I think Brandy already earned that one a long time ago." He paused and then added nervously, "From what I hear, that is."

I wasn't sure how to answer, so I didn't say anything. I thought it was sweet, though, that he didn't want me to think he'd personally partaken of Brandy's massage skills.

"So what time do you have to be home?" Brian said.

"No time, really. I've got some studying to do, but that can wait." In fact, the whole rest of my life could wait.

"Want to grab something to eat and then come to practice with me?"

Practice. It wasn't exactly what I'd imagined for an almost first date—Brian in his gym shorts throwing a ball around while I sit and watch. The gym shorts did add a positive spin to the whole thing, though. "Sure."

Lunch turned out to be a burger and fries in the car because Brian was late for practice. Since Brian paid, I wondered if this could be counted as our first date.

I found myself wondering the same thing a little while later as I sat in the bleachers, watching Brian bounce the basketball off the backboard and through the hoop.

"Are you going out with Brian?" A voice from behind me.

I spun around to find Daniel's sister, Brianna. She smiled at me.

"Um, no," I said, startled by her bluntness. "He just asked me to watch practice."

Brianna laughed. "That's a sign," she said.

"Of what?"

She climbed onto the bleachers and sat next to me. Then she leaned back and rested her elbows on the seat behind us. "The court is sacred," she said. "Players don't invite anyone to watch practice unless they think it'll bring them good luck."

"Really?" I said, feeling an involuntary smile coming on.

Brianna kicked her flip-flops off and let them fall under the bleachers. "Austin wouldn't let me come to practice for months. Then one day, I surprised him at the gym and he made two three-pointers. After that, I was a regular."

I looked around at the empty bleachers. "But isn't it boring after a while?"

"Sometimes," Brianna said. "But Randy and Ariana are usually here, too. We even have Cougar Girlfriend T-shirts." Then she added, "Mine's in the wash because I wore it yesterday."

I nodded. "Cool," I said, wondering exactly how cool it was to sit around an empty gym watching your boyfriend play basketball, wearing a shirt that defined you by your girlfriend status.

After a while Ariana and Randy showed up and sat in the row in front of us. Both looked a little surprised to see me. Randy gave me a scornful look and proceeded to talk only to Ariana. I'd expected them to leave *me* out of the conversation, but they didn't include Brianna either. It wasn't any great loss. They talked mostly about shoes and purses and the weekend spa camp. After a while they got up and went outside.

I turned to Brianna. "Are you going to the spa camp, too?"

She shook her head. "My parents think it's ridiculous. It costs like eight hundred dollars for the weekend."

I noticed she never took her eyes off the court. I wondered if I was breaking any of the "girlfriend" rules by not paying attention so I decided to focus on the practice. A lot of the guys had their shirts off. No wonder Brianna kept her eyes there.

I couldn't figure her out. She was a cheerleader and Austin's girlfriend, but she didn't seem to have much in common with the other "Cougar Girlfriends," despite the Stepford Wife T-shirt. I knew she got good grades because at a school like Crestview you know things like that. And she worked as a Latin tutor to freshmen. Daniel's big brother routine must have been paying off. There was more to her than shoes and spas.

I thought about my psych homework waiting for me at home and tried to pay attention to what was happening on the court. The guys were playing against each other—shirts against shirtless. Too bad Brian was on the shirts side. I hadn't had a peek at those abs since I'd delivered the captain's note. Was it possible that was only a week ago? Since then, I'd been hauled off to jail, gone to an athlete/cheerleader party, and had a sort of lunch date with Brian. Matchmaking for the elderly was definitely paying off.

Okay, focus on the game. Brian caught the ball, dribbled, and then tried for a long shot and missed. Austin took it on the rebound, shot, and made it. Then he looked up at Brianna to make sure she'd seen. Brianna let out the appropriate "woo-hoo," and Austin went back to the game. Funny. That was the kind of thing I'd seen my brother do with my mom.

It was Brian's ball again, but this time he passed it to Austin, who missed. "Out!" Coach Maxwell yelled when the ball landed on the other side of the painted red line. Brian and Austin looked down and shook their heads.

Ariana and Randy returned and continued to ignore us. They seemed to be following that unwritten cheerleader rule to keep your eyes on the court.

It wasn't like I had anything against cheerleaders, not all of them anyway. But I'd been brainwashed by my mom at an early age to find other activities. "Do something that'll make people cheer for *you*," she said.

I hadn't found out what that would be yet. But I still wondered why anyone would spend time off from school, cheering at a practice.

Then Brian made a three-pointer, turned to look up at me, and gave me the biggest smile ever. Suddenly, I understood why "Cougar Girlfriends" would spend their Sundays in the gym.

"Woo-hoo," I yelled.

FOURTEEN

Emily Moves Closer

"So what did you do all day?" my mother asked as she sliced a bright red tomato into perfect sections.

"Is that tomato for us or a photo shoot?"

Mom laughed. "Sometimes the food is actually for us to eat. I'm making a salad and your dad's grilling some chicken and sweet potatoes outside."

"Cool, but it can't compete with pizza."

My mother tilted the cutting board and slid the tomatoes into a bowl of lettuce. "Few things can compete with pizza. But you didn't answer my question."

"Brian and I delivered his grandmother's note to the captain of the *Conga Queen*. We ate lunch and I watched his basketball practice. Then we came home."

I tried to contain my excitement as I spoke. There was no telling how my parents would react. It wasn't like we were the Montagues and the Capulets, but the Harringtons weren't exactly on my mother's Christmas cookie list either.

Mom ran water over the cutting board, washing the leftover tomato seeds into the sink. "So you're serious about this matchmaking thing?"

"What do you mean serious?"

"Just that it's a big responsibility."

"How?" I hadn't thought delivering a few notes would be that much responsibility. It would have to end sometime. I mean, wouldn't Lily and Captain Miguel want to meet each other eventually? Or exchange phone numbers? Who knows? Maybe the captain even had a screen name. Lily could use Brian's computer, and she and Captain Miguel could IM each other. Put me right out of the message-distribution business.

Mom hesitated. "What if when they meet each other, one of them doesn't like the other one? Or one of them ends up heartbroken? Will you be ready to pick up the pieces?"

I hadn't thought of that. Was I ready to go from courier to consoler? Did I have the necessary skills to mend a broken heart? Especially a heart that had been around for a while? "Mom, you're freaking me out. I never thought of those things." What I didn't tell her was that the only thing I'd been thinking about was Brian.

"So what happened after you gave him the note?"

I picked up the dish towel and twirled it. "The captain gave me another note for Lily."

Mom shook her head. "I don't know about this. Do you have any idea what the note says?"

"Of course not. It's folded in the shape of a boat." Then I added, "Would a stalker or serial killer take the time to make a little paper boat?"

Mom frowned. "I don't know." She poured vinegar and then some olive oil into a bottle. "It's just that Lily might be a very lonely woman. Her judgment could be clouded when it comes to men. Are you sure you should deliver this note?"

The oil and vinegar bubbled as my mother shook the bottle. "I already said I'd deliver it later tonight." I paused. "I think I should keep my word." But was it my word or my date with Brian that I was really worried about keeping?

I waited until I saw the Harringtons' car leave the garage before I bounded downstairs and out the kitchen door that evening. Brian was already outside, bouncing a basketball on the driveway.

"Good timing," he said.

I smiled. It's easy to have good timing when you've

been waiting for forty-five minutes by your bedroom window.

Brian dribbled a few more times and tossed the ball against the backboard. It ricocheted and headed my way. I caught it and passed it to Brian. He passed it back. "Take a shot," he said. "We'll do a little one on one."

I dribbled a few times and shot from the side. My "sweet spot." I knew nothing about sports but somehow when I played basketball with my brother, I was always able to make a basket from that angle. "Yes!" I shouted as the ball went through the hoop.

"Not bad," Brian said. "A girl who can shoot a basket. Maybe Grams was right."

"What do you mean?"

Brian took a few more shots. "She said you were the perfect girl for me."

I caught the ball on the rebound and dribbled. Be cool. Be cool. Dribble the ball like you're not totally losing it. "Do you believe everything Grams says?"

Brian stole the ball from me and laughed. "Almost."

"So," I stammered, changing the subject before I made a complete fool of myself, "is Grams waiting for us?"

Brian hesitated. "I didn't mention it to her. I really wanted you to come over tonight, but I'm still not sure it's a good idea to give Grams the note—maybe we should read it first."

I'd been all for privacy before, but Brian seemed nervous. "Okay," I said. "I guess we could—just to make sure it doesn't say anything that could upset her."

I took out the note and unfolded it. It had gotten dark so Brian and I stepped onto the porch. The frogs, hidden away in the night, whirred around us as we stood under the lamplight. Brian's shoulder touched my cheek lightly and I tried to keep my hands from trembling as we read:

Dear Miss Lily,

I am wondering if you would do me the honor of joining me for dinner next Sunday. Please, if this is acceptable to you.

Your admiring fan,
Captain Miguel Velasquez

We stood there for a long time, as if we each had to sound out the words syllable by syllable, neither of us breaking apart. I felt the warmth of Brian's breath on my arm as my blood raced through me. It was as if nothing else existed—like it was just Brian and me, reading the note inside one of his parents' snow globes.

"Awww," I finally said in a whisper. "That's so cute. He's such a gentleman. Shall we give it to her now?"

Brian shrugged. "I guess it'll be okay if he took her

out to dinner. It's her decision anyway, right?"

"Right."

Once we were all in the cottage, Brian relaxed a little. Lily poured us some green tea. "What brings you here again?" she said.

"We delivered your note to the captain," I answered.

Lily's eyes sparkled. "You did? And what did he say?"

I produced the note that Brian and I had been unable to refold into its original boat shape but had just neatly folded into a square. Lily took it and read aloud to us, her voice cracking at the end. "How lovely," she said. And then she folded the note in half and put it on the table.

I wasn't sure if Lily intended to go on about the note, because the telephone interrupted us. Lily looked at it but didn't even bother to go over to the table. She looked at me and smiled. "We share a telephone line, but it's always for Brian."

Brian looked at the caller ID. "I'll call him back from my cell." Then he disappeared, leaving Lily and me alone with the captain's letter. How would I ever begin to have a relationship with Brian if he kept getting phone calls?

"So, Emily, what do you think of this Captain Miguel? He's not one of those older men who still thinks he's twenty, is he? You know with the shirt unbuttoned to his navel and the gold necklaces?"

"Um, no," I said, wondering in what universe twenty-year-old guys dressed like that.

"Is he a nice man?"

"I think so."

She leaned back on the couch. "You know, I had a wonderful relationship with my husband. We were the best of friends. We loved to go to the theater, the opera. But we also had our own interests. I had my dance classes and my charity work. But when my husband died, I wasn't prepared for the void in my life. That's when I decided to move to Florida—to be with my son and his family."

"I'm sorry," I whispered.

Lily patted my knee. "Don't be sorry, dear, they're not *that* horrible to live with."

"I didn't mean about your family," I said quickly. "I meant your husband."

"That's okay—I have lovely memories."

"But that void," I said. "Couldn't the captain fill just a tiny bit of it?" They did seem like a perfect match now that I thought about it. Both gave off a not-really-living-in-the-real-world vibe. "I could give him your phone number. Then the phone *would* be for you once in a while."

Lily smiled. "That would be a change, wouldn't it?" She paused, then added. "You're sure he's a nice man?"

"I'm pretty sure," I said. "But just in case, you

should meet him in a public place."

Lily's eyes met mine and began to twinkle. "You're a pretty smart girl, aren't you?"

"It's just what my mother always taught me. You know, don't go off with strangers. Make sure your cell phone is charged when you go out . . ."

Lily chuckled. "Now that's a new one. We always made sure we had a dime for a pay phone."

I smiled and then looked at my watch, wondering how long I should wait for Brian.

As if she were reading my mind, Lily announced, "I'll make more tea. We can chat until Brian comes back." She filled a pot with water and set it on the burner. "So dear, what do you do with your free time when you're not in school?"

I didn't want to tell her exactly how many hours of my life were devoted to daydreaming, particularly since my daydreaming happened to involve her grandson. "I work on the school newspaper," I said. "Right now I'm working on an article about the junior prom."

Lily took a pot holder out of a drawer. "Hmm," Lily said. "I don't think I've ever been to a prom. We had dances in my day, but no prom."

"Really?" I said. "I thought proms had been around forever." As soon as I spoke, I wanted to take the words back. I hoped she didn't think I meant *she'd* been around forever.

The teakettle let out a piercing whistle. "You know, I always thought it would be exciting to be a journalist," Lily said. "What will you write about the prom?"

So far all Daniel had was a list and I hadn't come up with anything else. "Right now we're thinking about doing it on how expensive everything is."

"Oooh," Lily said, her eyes getting wide. "An exposé. Just like *60 Minutes*!"

I hadn't thought of it that way, but it definitely made me feel better about the whole thing. "I guess so," I said.

Lily poured more tea. "So then how will you stop this prom nonsense?"

Stop it? Nonsense? What was she talking about? "Um, we don't want to stop the prom. We just want to write about how expensive it is!"

"Good journalists tell their readers how to change things," Lily said. "Otherwise, what good are the words?"

Ms. Keenan just assigned stories. She never said anything about giving instructions with them. "What do you mean?" I said.

Lily shuffled some newspapers on the glass coffee table and pointed to an article. "I just read this wonderful column. The writer told about how he was chastised by readers because when he wrote about how awful things were in countries like Africa, he never told readers what they could do about it."

I remembered the night of the attempted oakicide, when Daniel had said it wasn't our job to stop them from cutting the tree down. "But he's a journalist," I said. "He's supposed to just write the stories."

"Well, his readers complained that the problem with journalists is that they tell you what's wrong so they can feel good about themselves. But then the reader feels guilty." She paused. "So, do you want your readers to feel guilty about spending a lot of money at the prom? Or do you want them to do something about it?"

The answer was obvious. "But what could I possibly say that would make readers do anything about the cost of the junior prom? I can't see the Clausen twins and their friends shopping for gowns at the thrift store to save money. And even if they did, what good would it do?"

Lily rubbed her chin. "You're right. I've met the Clausens and their girls, and I can't picture them giving up a chance to spend money. But surely you can think of something that some of your friends could do to stop this ridiculousness."

By now my head was hurting. I understood what Lily was trying to say, but she clearly did not understand the students of Crestview Prep. Prom was a sacred ritual. Parents planned prom parties for weeks. Groups of kids met at one house to pick up the limo, while their parents took pictures and feasted on buffet dinners. It wasn't just the students that got excited about prom. Everyone did.

I was beginning to wish I'd never come over to the Harringtons; my homework was waiting. Brian was gone. And Lily was making me feel guilty and I wasn't even sure why. So when the door of the cottage opened, I jumped at the chance to leave.

"I'm sorry," Brian said sheepishly. "It was Austin. I couldn't get him off the phone."

Well, at least he'd tried to hurry.

"Want something to eat?" Brian said. "I think there's some key lime pie in the fridge."

"Sure." I looked at Lily. "It was nice talking to you. And thank you for the tea."

Lily folded the newspaper and placed it on top of a neat pile. "Lovely talking to you, my dear."

We were almost out the door when Lily added, "Oh, I almost forgot . . ." She took a deep breath and smoothed out the wrinkles in her floral top. "I've decided I'd like to meet Captain Miguel. Will you tell him I'd love to have dinner with him?"

Brian looked down at his sneakers and didn't say a word.

"Sure," I said. "If that's what you want, I'll tell him."

Lily ripped a piece of paper off a ladybug pad hanging on the wall and wrote the phone number on it. She started to hand it to me, but then stopped and said, "How silly of me. You probably know it already."

"No." I avoided looking at Brian. Of course I knew his number. I'd looked it up in the school directory and memorized it as soon as I'd started daydreaming about those eyes and that dimple. But I took the number from Lily as if it were the first time I was seeing it.

Brian put his hand on the small of my back as we walked across the patio to the house. The pool glistened as the water from the stone fountain spilled into it. Despite the warmth in the air, my skin tingled with goose bumps.

Brian took the pie out and set it on the table. "Just a tiny slice," I said. It was a bit unnerving to be alone in the Harrington house with Brian. "I'm still full from dinner. My dad barbecued."

"I know," Brian said. "It smelled good."

I watched him stab a piece of pie. "You should have come over," I said.

Brian smiled. "Maybe next time."

I sensed the whole pie and barbecue chatter was just small talk before something big was about to happen. I just didn't know how that thing was going to happen.

I took a bite of pie. It was sweet at first, then a little tart on the sides of my tongue. After Brian finished his last bite, he escorted me into the family room and onto a black leather couch. He turned on a basketball game but muted the sound, turning sideways to look at me. "I can't believe we lived next door to each other all this time and never hung out," he said.

Oh my God. This was definitely pre–making out banter. I recognized it from movies.

"Yeah," I said. "I know." From the corner of my eye, I watched a player dribble from one end of the court to the other. As he reached the basket, Brian's arm slipped around my shoulders and pulled me closer to him. The guy with the ball jumped in the air and dunked it into the basket.

Score! Brian's lips were suddenly on mine. I wrapped my arms around his neck and tasted the sweetness of graham cracker crust on his lips. Suddenly my body felt like the water from the fountain, falling and melting into a shimmering pool. Was this really happening? Oh my God! Was I really kissing Brian Harrington? And, more importantly . . . was I doing it right?

When we both needed a breath, we separated slightly but kept our foreheads touching. "We should definitely hang out more," Brian whispered.

"Definitely," I whispered back.

FIFTEEN

Emily on Detour?

"Whoa!" Lindsay said. "This is so surreal. What base did you get to?"

"Base? No one talks about bases anymore. You really are stuck in the fifties."

Lindsay took the aluminum foil off her tuna wrap. "I am not—I'm stuck in the sixties. That's much cooler. So then what happened?"

"We were on the couch for a while, and then we heard the garage door open and his parents' car pull in." I leaned closer to Lindsay. The lunchroom had begun to fill up, and people were headed toward our table. "Then we kind of collected ourselves and Brian walked me to my front yard."

Lindsay shook her head. "What a difference a week makes, huh? Last Sunday night you were stalking him, and a week later you're—"

"So, Woodward, you come up with an angle for the prom story yet?" an annoying voice interrupted.

Lindsay looked up at Daniel and then at me. "Woodward?"

"It's just Daniel's lame attempt at humor," I said. "He doesn't think I can come up with the kind of hard-hitting investigative piece about the prom that he came up with." I glared at him. "Now what was your idea? 'Prom: It's Expensive!' I don't know if I can top that."

Daniel grinned. "Laugh if you will, but if you don't come up with something else by two o'clock today, we're going with it." He proceeded to hum the theme song from the final question on *Jeopardy* as he strolled away.

"Grrrr." I broke a piece of my peanut butter and jelly sandwich off and threw it on the table. "He acts so superior. I can't stand it."

"Whoa, sandwich that bad, huh?"

I spun around to find Brian smiling at me. I was sure my face was the color of the jelly I'd just tossed onto the table.

"Hey," Brian said. "I was hoping I'd see you. Want to come to practice later?"

I bit my lip. "Um, I have to work on my newspaper

article this afternoon. We've got a deadline."

Austin walked by and jutted his chin out to show Brian where the team was sitting. It was almost a mandate that Brian sit with them. He nodded and then turned to me. "Maybe I'll see you later at home?"

"Sure," I said, wishing I could just blink my eyes and make it later right away.

Ms. Keenan peeked over our shoulders as Daniel and I sat at the computer. "Have you come up with an angle for the prom story yet?"

Daniel and I looked at each other. I began to stammer. "We . . . um . . ."

Daniel finished the sentence for me. "In a couple of minutes." Ms. Keenan nodded and walked away.

"What?" I whispered furiously. "We're not ready."

Daniel pointed to Ethan Rose and Carly Kendrick. Carly was typing away and Ethan was reading from notes next to her. "They're our competition," Daniel said, "for the coeditors position next year."

"Coeditors?"

"I overheard Ms. Keenan talking to another teacher and found out that whoever comes up with the best angle on a prom story gets the front page in the next issue of the *Crestview Courier*—and the coeditor position."

"You have *got* to be kidding. We may as well give up now."

Carly Kendrick's family owned a fleet of limousines, among other things, and was even wealthier than Austin's family. They gave tons of money to the school, and Carly was handsomely rewarded with leadership positions and coveted roles in musicals. Despite the fact that she couldn't carry a tune—even if it was tucked inside her Burberry bag. Ethan was a favorite of the administration because he was a champion debater. Anyone who could fill the hallway cabinets with trophies always had an edge.

I dropped my forehead into my hands. "We are so doomed."

Daniel frowned. "I didn't figure you for someone who would give up that easily."

I looked down at my notebook and then over at Daniel's. "What do we have? You've got a shopping list and I've got . . ." I opened my notebook to where I'd written, "*The History of Proms*."

"The history of proms?" Daniel said, his voice stinking of sarcasm. "What is this, an AP course? That'll really grab the few people who actually read the articles instead of just scanning for sports scores."

I looked down at the words. "It sounded like a good idea last night when I wrote it."

I didn't want to tell Daniel that after I left Brian's house, everything sounded like a good idea. I could have written "Serial Killers and Proms" and it would have sounded absolutely brilliant to me. Then I remembered why I had written about the history of proms. Lily mentioned they hadn't had proms in her day. I was just about to explain my idea, when Ms. Keenan came back. "Ready?" she said.

Daniel ripped the page out of his notebook and handed it to her. "It's about the gross materialism of prom."

Ms. Keenan nodded.

I tore the page out of my notebook and almost flung it at her. "And the history of it," I added. "How prom has changed over the years to become this gigantic, expensive ritual." Then I heard Lily's voice in my head and proceeded to spout off the top of my head. "But we can't just write it and make people feel guilty. We have to tell them what they can do about it."

Daniel's eyes widened and he mouthed, "What?"

"You've raised a very good point," Ms. Keenan said.

I gave Daniel a smug smile.

Then she continued, "Good journalism should inspire readers. So what suggestions will you have for them?"

My eyes met Daniel's and we both stared blankly for a minute.

"Suggest they skip the junior prom altogether," Daniel blurted.

Now it was his turn to return the smug smile as my mouth dropped open. "Are you crazy?" I said.

"That would certainly make a statement," Ms. Keenan said. "But how many people do you think would go along with that?"

I shrugged. "About three. You can't ask kids to give up the prom." Or ask me to give up my chance of going to the prom with Brian Harrington.

"It's just the *junior prom,*" Daniel said. "It's not like we're suggesting everyone go crazy and give all their possessions to the poor. They'll have next year's prom to do it up big."

Ms. Keenan turned to Daniel. "I don't know. Emily does have a point. You can't ask your fellow classmates to give up the prom entirely. But you could suggest a less expensive, alternative prom—I've heard about kids from other schools doing that." Ms. Keenan paused. "But I'm still not sure what kind of statement you'd be making."

"And even if kids spend less money on an alternative prom, what good would it do?" Daniel said. "They'd just spend it on other stuff."

There was no going back now and I suddenly had an idea. "We could make it a fund-raiser. We'll sell tickets and use some of the money for our alternative prom and donate the rest to a good cause."

Daniel's face brightened. "We could give the money to Mount Saint Mary's Nursing Home—for their own prom."

Ms. Keenan smiled. "Sounds like a plan. You've got till Wednesday to work out all the details and write the article." Then she put a hand on each of our shoulders. "Good work, you two."

Everything had happened so fast, I wasn't sure what Daniel and I had agreed to. I was glad it sounded so impressive, but I wasn't sure how we were going to pull the whole thing off. My eyes followed Ms. Keenan over to Ethan and Carly. I didn't know what angle they'd come up with, but I was pretty sure canceling the junior prom wouldn't be it.

I was trying to read their lips when Daniel tapped me on the shoulder. "Do you realize what we've done?"

I glared at him. "What do you mean *we*? Skip the junior prom? What were you thinking?"

Daniel cocked his head. "Oh yeah. Blame it all on me, Miss Brownnoser. What was that whole thing about how we need to tell people what to do about it and not just make them feel guilty? We never discussed *that* together."

I lowered my eyes. I didn't want to tell him I'd gotten the idea from Brian's grandmother. Instead, I said, "Remember the night we got arrested? You were starting to agree with me that sometimes it's a journalist's job to take action, right?"

Daniel narrowed his eyes. "I guess we have no choice now, do we?"

We ignored each other's presence as we sat, jotting ideas down in our notebooks. I could hear the scratching of Daniel's pen taunting me.

"Okay," he said. "How about this for a lead?" He read it aloud: "'For years Crestview Cougars have been spending thousands of dollars on the junior prom. Now it's time to spend it on the senior prom. No, not that senior prom. The real seniors over at Mount Saint Mary's Nursing Home.'"

"It's clever," I said. "But do we even know they'd want a prom?"

"Ten bucks says they'd love it," Daniel said. "Did you see how excited they were when we played the piano? And we sucked." He folded his notebook and stuck it in his backpack. "Ms. Keenan," he called across the room. "Emily and I are leaving to do research for the article. Okay with you?"

Ms. Keenan smiled and waved.

How did he get away with that stuff?

"Where are we going?" I demanded as I followed Daniel into the parking lot.

"To win me ten bucks."

"Wait a minute," I said. "I didn't take that bet."

"Okay, you're right. But we've got to get going on this. The prom's in less than three weeks. We can't ask people to give it up unless we've got a definite plan."

I slid into the front seat of Daniel's car and wondered what I was getting myself into.

❀ ❀ ❀

"You're doing what?" my dad said.

I scooped some black beans on top of the rice that was already in my dish. "An alternative junior prom," I said. "We set it all up today with the people at Mount Saint Mary's. We'll split the money we make in ticket sales to finance a junior prom for Crestview and another one for the residents at the nursing home."

My dad shook his head. "I don't know."

As an accountant, my father is a very practical man. He thinks in terms of profits and losses and I'm sure the words "alternative prom" read "big loss" to him.

"You know, the school could lose money on this. They have accounts with hotels and caterers and photographers . . ."

"But it's for charity," I said. "The school should be happy about that."

My father laughed. "The school is a business, Em."

"Well, I think it's a great idea," my mom said. "Your father forgets when he was in college, he was an activist."

"Really?" I said. I'd seen pictures of my father with long hair and funny, wire-rimmed glasses, which were very un-accountant-like, but I'd never heard about any type of activism. "What did you do?"

My parents looked at each other and then over at my brother and me. "I guess it's okay to tell you now," my father said. "I was arrested at a sit-in, trying to close a draft board. We were protesting the Vietnam War."

"Wow!" my brother shouted. I was pretty sure he had no idea what a draft board was, but the thought of my father getting arrested seemed way cool to him. He looked at my mom. "And you got mad at me last week because my book report was a week late?"

My mother put down her chicken wing and frowned at him. "That was procrastination—not politics." She turned to me. "If you really believe in this, I think you should do it."

My father must have gone into a reverie about the good old days because after a few minutes he agreed with her. "You can even use the backyard for the alternative prom," he said. "One of my clients has a party company; maybe I can get him to donate a tent and some tables and chairs."

My mother pointed to the chicken, rice, beans, and fried bananas on the table. "Casa Pollo is a client of mine. I'm sure they'll donate the food for such a good cause."

"Great," I said. "But I want to hear more about Dad's arrest."

My father wiped his chin with a napkin. "Maybe another day."

My mother began to clear the table. "I'm really proud of you," she said. "Remember how you told me one time that you wanted to take the world by storm?"

I looked up and caught a glimpse out the kitchen window behind her. Brian was out there shooting baskets with Luis and Austin. "Speaking of storms, can I take a rain check on this conversation?" I said. "I've got to tell Brian something."

My mother smiled. "Just don't be long. I've got the feeling homework hasn't exactly been a priority these days."

Was it that obvious? As I walked across the yard, the tips of the tall grass stung my ankles.

Brian tossed the ball to Luis and met me halfway.

"Hey," I said. "Still practicing, huh?"

"Getting ready for the big game."

"Great," I said. I had no idea what team they were playing. I just knew it was somewhere in the middle of the state and Brian would be away for the weekend. "I wanted to let you know that I gave Captain Miguel your grandmother's phone number today," I said.

"You did? When did you see him?"

"I was on my way to research an article for the school newspaper and passed by the place where the *Conga Queen* docks. I took a chance and stopped. The captain was there so I gave him the number." I avoided mentioning I was with Daniel at the time. "I don't know if you want to tell Lily. Maybe you want her to be surprised." My sentences were punctuated by the sound of the basketball hitting the backboard every few seconds.

"Wow," Brian said. "Grams on a date. That should put my mother over the edge. She's been trying to get Grams to stop dancing in the backyard for a couple of years. This'll give them a whole new thing to argue about."

"Will it be a problem?"

"Oh yeah, definitely. But I'm out of it, so it's okay."

I nodded. "Well, good, then. I'll let you get back to your game."

"Thanks," he said and then added with a smile, "Maybe we can get together later."

I hesitated. Daniel and I had only two more days to get the alternative prom details worked out and write the story. But finally, after all this time, I had a chance with the boy next door! What a choice: Brian and his abs or Daniel and his arrogance. But a deadline was a deadline. "I've got a lot of homework tonight. Maybe tomorrow night?"

"Sure," Brian said. He actually looked a little disappointed.

"So Frances seemed pretty excited about the nursing home prom," I said, kicking off my shoes and plopping down in front of the computer. After our trip to Mount Saint Mary's, Daniel and I had agreed to work on the article together over the phone.

"Told you she would," he said.

I ignored his told you so. "You realize we now have to write the article and then plan two proms?"

"We can do it," Daniel said. "You want to type and we'll write it together now?"

It wasn't my idea of a fun night, given the alternative, but it was what I had to do. I was surprised at how quickly the time went. And I had to admit, despite Daniel's puns, he was a pretty good writer. By the time I looked at the clock, it was almost midnight. We'd gotten all the details worked out and a rough draft of the article written. We planned to polish it the next day and turn it in on Wednesday. Then set the wheels in motion for the Support-the-Alternative-Prom campaign.

I was one step closer to my master plan. My dream of being Brian Harrington's prom date actually had a shot at coming true, but so what if we didn't go to the regular prom together? We'd be the king and queen of the alternative prom.

SIXTEEN

Emily's Direction Uncertain

The next night, I found myself standing next to Lily in front of a closet full of polyester pants and shiny tops. "They sparkle when the boats shine their lights on me," she explained.

"I'm sure the captain will like any of these," I said, feeling as if I were suddenly starring in a reality show called *Style for Seniors*. The captain had wasted no time getting in touch with Lily. Their Sunday dinner date was already planned.

"You'll look great, Grams," Brian said from the couch.

It wasn't like I didn't want Lily to look nice, but I couldn't wait to be alone with Brian. I pulled out a pair of brown pants and a pink top with brown trim that had a minimum of sparkles. "I think he'll like this one."

Lily examined it and agreed. "You'll be here when the captain comes?" she asked again.

I nodded. The Harringtons were driving to Lakeland for the big game, so I had agreed to come over beforehand. The captain would pick Lily up at four to catch the early bird special at the Sea View. I figured it would be a fitting end to my matchmaking career for the aged.

"Okay then," Lily said. "You two run along."

I tried to contain my excitement as Brian and I almost raced to the Harrington family room. This time Brian skipped the formality of offering food and we went straight to the couch. He'd mentioned earlier that his parents had gone out for a quick dinner and they weren't too happy about what they called my "do-it-yourself-dating-service"—which really did not have a nice ring to it. Part of me wanted to leave the Harrington house as fast as I could, but then there was that other part that wanted to feel the cool leather couch against my arms and legs and Brian's hot lips against mine.

And because it was dark and I was dazed and I was obviously experiencing the pheromones present in Brian's basketball sweat, I don't think I can be blamed for what happened next.

As Brian's lips moved closer to mine, between warm

breaths, he uttered the words, "Hey, do you want to go to the prom with me?"

I suddenly understood the phrase, *"in the heat of the moment."* Because in the heat of that moment, all I could think of was Brian's lips nearing mine and wanting them to reach their destination and if I said no, those lips would stop being there and everything would be ruined. So I did it. I took a breath and said, "Yes."

Not long after that, the roar of the Harringtons' Mercedes pulling into the garage jolted me back to reality. Brian quickly escorted me out the back way and kissed me at the gate.

Later, as I got ready for bed, I alternated between feeling a giddy delight that I might be dating Brian Harrington, and the horrible realization that I'd agreed to go to a prom that I was boycotting. What was I going to do?

I saw Brian for only a few minutes before the bus took off for state on Friday morning. Then Daniel and I kicked off the Support-the-Alternative-Prom campaign during lunch.

As Daniel and I sat in front of the cafeteria with a stack of tickets he'd printed on his computer, I heard Brandy Clausen's voice. "I heard the reason she's doing it is because her butt was too big to fit into any prom dresses."

My jaw tightened. I admit I once got stuck in one of those slinky, silvery gowns in the dressing room at Prom World. And it did take three other girls to get it off me and I was almost decapitated in the process. But the same thing happened to Lindsay right afterward and she's an absolute stick. So I really resented that rumor. A lot.

It turned out Brandy's voice was the first of many who did not share our enthusiasm for charitable events. Occasionally someone would stop and ask what the tickets were for. We got a lot of eye rolling and head shaking when we explained that for thirty dollars they'd be getting an alternative prom in my backyard and a "good feeling" that they were supporting a prom for senior citizens.

Finally some guy I didn't know picked up a ticket and reached into his pocket. Daniel and I looked at each other with anticipation. Our first sale.

The guy scribbled on the ticket and then flicked it back at us. He'd crossed out the word "support" and written "sucks" after "Alternative Prom."

"Nice," Daniel said, as the guy walked away.

"Real mature," I yelled after him.

Later in the parking lot, when Lindsay asked how sales went, I admitted we hadn't sold one ticket.

"But it's only the first day," I added quickly. "Maybe you can get some of your friends from the Crestview

Choir to come? Don't they all want to be music majors in college? They may as well get used to not spending a lot of money."

"I'll try," Lindsay said. "I'll talk it up next week." She was quiet for a second and then her face brightened. "Hey, maybe you can get Brian and the whole basketball team to support the alternative prom. Then everyone would come."

I looked down at the gravel. I'd never gotten the chance to tell Brian about the alternative prom. I tried to convince myself he wouldn't care which prom he went to as long as it was with me. But I had no idea how he'd react when I told him.

"I haven't exactly told Brian about the alternative prom, yet," I ventured.

"What?" Lindsay cried.

"Well . . ." I hesitated. "It gets worse. Last night, he asked me to the *regular* prom, and I couldn't think straight. I just said yes."

"So," Lindsay said, "let me get this right: Brian thinks you're going to the regular prom with him and Daniel thinks you're going to the alternative prom with him."

"What? I'm not going to the alternative prom with Daniel. Is that what he thinks?"

"I don't know," Lindsay said. "It's just that, you know, it's your project together and . . ." She fiddled with her backpack zipper.

I grabbed her arm. "If you know something that you're not telling me . . ."

She hesitated. "I've been looking at his blog and . . ."

"You read his blog?"

"It's pretty funny," Lindsay continued. "But recently he's been kind of serious. He put up this link to a site about male/female relationships."

"What does it say?"

"Something about how girls never fall for the guys they're friends with; they only like guys that are inconsiderate, that are into themselves, what he calls 'prom king types.'"

"That is so not true!"

"Well, it seems Daniel is a proponent of the theory and I don't know why he'd care except—"

"Except what?"

"If he's really talking about you," Lindsay said.

"You're crazy," I shouted. Then I looked around and lowered my voice. "There is no way Daniel Cummings likes me that way. And no way I like him that way. He has no redeeming qualities at all." I thought for a minute. "The only good thing I can say about him is that he wears nice cologne—it smells kind of woodsy. But that's it."

Lindsay shook her head. "Guys are weird. Once at arts camp I had a duet partner who criticized my playing all the time and later I found out from this girl who played the bassoon that he really liked me."

"Well, I don't know what Daniel's thinking, but I'm going to the alternative prom with Brian and that's final."

Lindsay frowned at me.

"Um, that is, as soon as I tell him about it."

I admired Lily's blouse as she spun around, getting ready for her date with Captain Miguel.

"You know," Lily said. "I feel like I did on my first date with my husband, years ago."

"How did you meet him?"

"I was working as a dancer in New York City and I had lots of men trying to meet me. They would come to the back of the theater to get a glimpse of us dancers. We called them Stage-Door Johnnies. Lots of the girls went out with them because they were exciting. They wore expensive suits and drove fancy cars." She paused. "But there was this one man who was different. He came three nights in a row and brought me pink roses every time. And then he disappeared. I didn't see him anymore."

"What happened to him?"

Lily took a deep breath. "One day, I was walking down the street and I spotted him. I told him I'd missed him and we agreed to meet later at the coffee shop next to theater. When I showed up, there was a vase with a dozen pink roses sitting right in the middle of a table."

"But where had he been for all those months?" I said.

"That's the craziest thing," Lily said. "He felt he couldn't compete with all the men with their fancy cars and suits. But I told him I'd had enough of those men with their big egos."

"So did you get married soon after that first date?" I said.

Lily shook her head. "We became friends first and we got married a year later." She looked out the front window. "But that was a long time ago," she whispered.

When she turned around, her eyes were watery.

"Are you okay?" I said.

Lily wrung her hands. "I'm just a little nervous."

Then the doorbell rang. As Lily went to get it, I suddenly felt very protective of her. What was that line in *The Little Prince*? "You are responsible for what you tame?" Weren't you also responsible for what you set free? Lily had been cooped up for so long in the cottage behind the Harrington house. Sure, she danced for the boats, but was that enough?

Lily returned from the door with Captain Miguel by her side. She held a bouquet of flowers—no roses but a bunch of beautiful purple flowers. She winked as she passed me to get a vase from the kitchen. "Emily, could you help me?"

"Why didn't you tell me the captain was so handsome?" she whispered. "And so young?"

I didn't think Captain Miguel was either of those things, but I wasn't going to tell Lily that. "I knew that wouldn't matter to you," I said.

Lily placed the flowers in the vase and set them on the counter. She gave me a hug and whispered, "Thank you, Emily."

I hugged her back. "Do you have a dime for a phone call?" I teased and we both laughed. "Now go," I said. "Your date is waiting."

SEVENTEEN

Emily on Collision Course?

The Crestview hallways buzzed with excitement Monday morning after the big weekend win. The few Support-the-Alternative-Prom posters that Daniel and I had put up had been torn down to make room for Cougars-Take-State-by-Storm banners.

It reminded me of my junior year goals—I was so close to going to the prom with Brian and to the editor in chief position, too. But it seemed the two goals had suddenly become incompatible. Walking down the hall with Lindsay, I was deep in thought when I was suddenly swooped off my feet.

"We won!" Brian shouted as he spun me around in the air.

After two 360-degree spins, he placed me back on the ground. "I heard," I said, trying to regain my equilibrium. That whole spinning-in-the-air thing looked a lot better in commercials than it actually felt.

"My dad's getting me a new car 'cause we won," Brian said, smiling. "And that's not all; the parents got together after the game and decided they'd pay for a Hummer limo and a weekend on the beach after the prom. It's gonna be tight."

"Yeah," I said. "Tight," which was exactly the description of the grip Lindsay suddenly had on my arm. "But about the prom—"

Suddenly, a couple of basketball players pushed Brian from behind. He spun around, did some kind of weird handshake, and took off with them. As an afterthought, he yelled back, "Hey, I'll see you later."

Was the whole team attached at the hips?

"You know," Lindsay said, "it's like a teen sitcom where the girl tells two different boys she'll go to the prom with them and then she doesn't know what to do. But this is different. Your other date's a—"

"A whole other prom," I said, finishing her sentence. "It's like a bad sci-fi film—*When Proms Collide*. I can fulfill my dream of going with Brian. Or I can keep my promise to support the alternative prom." Why hadn't I just agreed with Daniel's *Prom*nivores idea?

Lindsay stopped in front of the staircase by her

homeroom. "Maybe Brian will want to go with you to the alternative prom?"

"Yeah," I said. "Who knows?"

"In the meantime," Lindsay said, "you'd better figure out how to tell him, because you're supposed to sell tickets at lunch today."

"So tell me about this alternative prom," a guy named Richard from my Latin class said as he picked up a ticket.

"We're protesting the materialism of the junior prom," Daniel said. "Buy a ticket to our less-expensive prom and not only will we guarantee a good time but you'll be supporting a worthy cause."

I was getting really tired of hearing Daniel's spiel. And I was beginning to doubt that whole "good time" part of the speech, too.

"What cause is that?" Richard asked.

"We're using the leftover money so the residents of Mount Saint Mary's Nursing Home can have a prom," I explained.

"Cool," he said, nodding his head.

Really? Did he say cool? Up until then, Daniel and I had sold exactly four tickets—to ourselves, Lindsay, and Natalia Dash, who was up for anything with the prefix anti-. She was antimeat, antipoultry. Why not antiprom?

"Some friends and I were going to have our own prom," Richard said. "To protest . . . you know, other traditions." Then he added, "It's not just a hetero thing is it?"

"Nope," Daniel answered. "Anyone's welcome. How many tickets do you want?"

Richard thought for a minute. "Put me down for seven—for the whole gay-straight alliance."

"We have a gay-straight alliance at Crestview?" I said. "Why haven't I ever heard of it?"

Richard laughed. "It's sort of low-key—mostly a bunch of friends getting together for dinner and hanging out. You're welcome to join us."

Daniel added Richard's name to our list and put a big seven next to it.

As Richard walked away, Daniel and I began a silent cheer—until we were interrupted by Kristin Turner's accusatory voice. "Are you both trying to win a Gold Sword award?"

It was a strange accusation from someone who entered every competition known to Crestview. She once entered a songwriting contest even though she never studied a day of music. With the odds on her side, she'd won some kind of award every year since first grade. I guessed we were treading on her territory.

Each year the school nominated two people who performed distinctive community service. Nominees from every school in the district were evaluated, and the two top contenders won scholarship money. The school got a lot of press and a big gold sword to display in the office.

"Uh, this might be a foreign concept to you, Kristin," Daniel said. "But sometimes people do good things just for the sake of doing them—not for an award or another line on their résumé."

Kristin huffed and walked away.

"What is her problem?" I said.

Daniel put the tickets back in the manila envelope along with the makeshift sign. "Who knows, but at least we're up to eleven tickets now."

I nodded. "Pretty good, huh?"

"It's not quite enough to fund Mount Saint Mary's prom and ours yet," Daniel said. He paused and then added with his familiar smirk, "Maybe you could get your friend Harrington and his buddies to come over to the dark side."

Somehow I'd managed to avoid Brian all day—even during the ticket sales at lunch. Cougar basketball mania had overshadowed anything else going on at Crestview, so it was a pretty good bet he and his friends still didn't know about the alternative prom. Nevertheless, I felt my face turn red. Did Daniel know about Brian asking me to the prom?

Could Brian have told Austin and then Austin told

Brianna? She did seem to have trouble keeping secrets. "Um, well, you know those guys. I don't know . . ."

Daniel shoved the envelope in his backpack. "I was just kidding. There's no way they'd give up a night of excess, not for anyone."

Was that some kind of challenge? "Maybe they'd do it for the right someone," I snapped.

Daniel shook his head. "Some traditions are tough to go up against—even for a hot girl with a social conscience." Then he turned to go up the stairs to his next class.

I was struck silent. Had Daniel Cummings just called me hot? I was surprisingly not repulsed.

By the time I arrived at the cottage, Brian and Lily were deep into a heated discussion.

"Sweetie," Lily said. "I can't let you do that."

"It's okay," Brian said. "There's no way Dad would let me quit basketball." Brian spun toward the door when it opened. He gave me a quick hug before motioning toward the couch where Lily was sitting. I was getting used to this easy familiarity we had when we saw each other.

"What's this about quitting basketball?" I said. I couldn't imagine a scenario that could make Brian give up the team.

"It's a ridiculous notion that Brian has," Lily said.

Brian shook his head in exasperation. "My parents don't want Grams to go out with the captain again. They think he's just looking to marry someone to stay in the country."

My mouth dropped open. Had my mother been right? Should I have checked things out before setting up the date? I turned to Lily for some sign that I hadn't done anything wrong.

"It's a bit insulting, isn't it?" she said. "The idea that a man would only be interested in me to get a green card."

I nodded. "Why do they think that?"

"When we got home from state, my parents met Captain Miguel. They noticed his accent and decided he must be illegal."

"Which is just ridiculous," Lily interjected. "He's been in this country for years."

"But how will Brian quitting basketball help?" I asked.

Lily put her arm around Brian. "He really is Sir Galahad after all, isn't he?" she said. "He wants to give his parents an ultimatum—if I can't see Captain Miguel, he'll quit basketball. But I can't let him do that."

"Grams," Brian said. "There's no way my dad would let me quit. We just won state. He's on a high. You should have seen him."

"But, dear, I don't want you to take that chance."

Brian turned to me. "What do you think?"

I was flustered. Should I take a side? What if I agreed and Brian's dad called his bluff? I ran the risk of incurring the wrath of the entire Crestview student body. Without Brian as point guard, who knows what would happen? But then I remembered. Taking a stand was my new thing. Standing up for the First Amendment. Standing up against the materialism of the prom. Funny how Daniel had influenced both. I didn't know whether to thank him or blame him. I looked at Lily. "Did you really like Captain Miguel?"

She practically glowed. "He's a wonderful man," she said. "So cultured. He even loves the ballet."

It wasn't easy finding a guy like that at any stage of life. Captain Miguel was a definite keeper. I looked at Brian and shrugged. "Seems like it's worth a try."

He broke into a big smile. "See, Grams—I'll tell him later tonight."

Grams shook her head. "I hope we're doing the right thing. I know how much you love basketball. I don't want you sacrificing that for me."

"Trust me," Brian said. "I know my dad."

I tried to think of something else to say in order to prolong the visit with Lily. I knew that as soon as we left, I had to tell Brian about the prom. I stalled as long as I could, pressing Lily for the details about her date.

But before long we'd gone all the way from the shrimp cocktail to the chocolate mousse. There was nothing left to tell.

We were on the couch when Brian put his hand on the back of my neck and pulled me toward him. But before our lips could touch, I blurted, "I have to tell you something."

He pulled away from me. "You don't want to kiss me?" he said.

"Oh no, that's not it," I said. "It's just that we have to talk." I hesitated. "About the prom."

"Oh that," Brian said. "Don't worry. Even though my parents are mad about the whole Captain Miguel thing, we can still go together."

Brian's parents hadn't even occurred to me. "It's not that," I said. "It's just that when you asked me, I sort of forgot that I'd made another commitment."

Brian was silent, but his eyes revealed he was hurt.

"Oh, I didn't mean another date," I said quickly. "It's just that, um, Daniel and I wrote this article for the *Crestview Courier* encouraging people to come to an alternative, less expensive prom, instead of the regular one."

Brian's eyebrows drew together. "I heard something about that today in school," he said. "Isn't that a gay thing?"

"No," I said. "It's a fund-raiser. We're using the extra money to have a prom for the old people at Mount Saint Mary's."

Brian was still frowning. "So you're having the prom at a nursing home?"

"One of them," I said. "The other one, for the juniors, will be in my backyard. My dad's getting a tent and chairs, and Casa Pollo is donating the food." Even as I rattled them off, I knew those things were unlikely to sell the idea. I mean, really. We were up against strapless evening gowns, limos, and hotels with no parental supervision. It wasn't much of a contest.

"Wow," Brian said. "So you can't go to those *and* the regular prom?"

I shook my head. "They're all on the same day. The nursing home prom's during the day so it doesn't interfere with their schedule. And the other one's at night. The same night as the regular prom."

Brian rubbed the back of his neck. "So what are you going to do?"

I looked down at the couch. "I don't know . . . maybe you could come with me to the alternative prom?"

Brian paused. "I don't know. The guys and I made these plans . . ."

"I know," I said.

"Couldn't you just let the others handle that alternative thing?" Brian pulled me toward him and pressed his lips against mine. They were soft and sweet and irresistible.

We parted and I took a deep breath. "Well, maybe the others could handle it."

EIGHTEEN

Emily Stays the Course

It had been a week since Daniel and I had turned in our article and started the whole alternative prom movement. But it seemed like months. In just two and a half weeks, I'd managed to:

1. Make a successful match between Lily and Captain Miguel
2. Almost get arrested with Daniel Cummings
3. Get Brian to ask me to the prom, thus fulfilling a long-held goal
4. Start an antiprom movement, thus jeopardizing the above long-held goal
5. Gotten closer to becoming editor in chief of the *Crestview Courier* (even if it was a coeditor position with Daniel Cummings)

And yet, I was no closer to achieving my larger ambition of taking the world by storm.

In fact, my life had become more like a series of confused funnel clouds bumping into each other in the atmosphere—if that was scientifically possible.

While I was reviewing for my psych exam in the cafeteria before school, it suddenly occurred to me that I was actually living out the types of conflict in the book.

Approach-approach conflict: I wanted to go the regular prom with Brian, but I also wanted to keep my word about supporting the alternative prom.

Approach-avoidance conflict: I wanted to do the right thing and go to the alternative prom, but I wanted to avoid losing Brian, which could happen.

Avoidance-avoidance conflict: I didn't want to tell Brian I couldn't go to the prom with him, and I also didn't want to tell Daniel that I was bailing on the alternative prom.

I was trying to figure out exactly what had gone wrong with my master plan when Lindsay walked by the table. "Have you told him yet?" Her eyes had an accusing look.

I bit my lip.

"You have to tell him today."

"I know, I know, but the minute I tell him I'll have to let go of my whole prom fantasy. It's like giving up the idea of Santa Claus."

Lindsay jokingly patted my shoulder. "You got over that and it's been okay, hasn't it?"

I pouted. "Yes, but I really miss Santa Claus."

Lindsay left for her locker while I stared down at my book. I was still feeling sorry for myself when Daniel dropped a newspaper on the table in front of me.

The leading headline: CRESTVIEW JUNIORS PLAN ALTERNATIVE PROM. And underneath: BY EMILY BENNET AND DANIEL CUMMINGS.

"Check it out," he said. "We're Bennet and Cummings—saving the world, one alternative prom ticket at a time."

"Whoa, cool. Where'd you get this?" I said.

"It's hot off the presses. Ms. Keenan just gave it to me."

"So where's the story Carly and Ethan wrote?"

"Buried on page eight. The competition wasn't even close. They wrote some unoriginal article about how to have the 'best' prom experience. Where to find the best clothes, the best hotel, the best *limo*."

"Ha," I said. "Wonder which limo service they recommended."

Daniel laughed. "We've got that coeditor position in the bag."

"You think?"

"Definitely," Daniel said. Then he got serious for a second and added, "That's the good news."

"There's bad news?" I said, bracing myself.

Daniel frowned. "Ms. Burns wants to see us in her office."

"Again?" I had successfully avoided any principal's office in more than eleven years. But since my acquaintance with Daniel, I'd become a regular—visiting for the second time in less than three weeks.

Ms. Burns sat across from us with her birdlike face looking pointier than usual. "It has come to my attention," she said, "that the two of you are plotting to boycott the junior prom."

I'd previously thought the word *plot* was reserved for talking about novels and assassinations, not fundraising events. But Ms. Burns seemed to think otherwise. She continued, "I believed you two had learned your lesson after the display at Saint Bart's."

I was stunned. Suddenly, Daniel and I were the bad guys again.

"You know the members of the board of trustees have many business acquaintances who benefit from both the junior and senior proms: hotel owners, caterers, florists, limousine services. While I appreciate your desire to perform a service to the community, we can't go upsetting the apple cart because a few students don't want to go to the prom."

What? If she only knew how much I *wanted* to go to the prom. How desperately I wanted to be Brian Harrington's date. I was giving up my entire junior year fantasy and she was upset because Carly Kendrick's father might lose a couple of limo deals.

In between my thoughts and rage, I heard Daniel's voice. "Ms. Burns," he said, "with all due respect to the apple cart . . ."

Oh no! Was Daniel going to mess this up even more with his sarcasm?

". . . we had no intention of upsetting the board of trustees. We're on your side. Emily and I were hoping our community service project would put the spotlight on how compassionate the students are at Crestview—you know, in addition to being smart and athletic."

What? I glared at him.

Ms. Burns's eyes widened.

Daniel leaned closer to her. "We were hoping to win a Gold Sword award for the school." So that's what he was planning—to stab me in the back with a Gold Sword. I could almost feel the blade.

Ms. Burns straightened in her seat. I imagined the inside of her mouth, salivating at the mention of the Gold Sword.

Daniel folded his hands on her desk and smiled. Her face softened. She opened a drawer to her left and pulled out some papers.

"Well then," she said, handing them to Daniel. "Fill out these award applications and return them to me so I can process them."

She handed Daniel the applications and we got up to leave the office. I was happy to be getting out of there, but something inside me felt sick to think that Daniel had been playing me all along. I was positive he'd been sincere about the alternative prom.

Once we were outside the main office, I turned to him. He had that grin on his face that I hated. "What was all that about the Gold Sword?" I said. "What happened to 'sometimes people do good things just for the sake of doing them'?"

Daniel laughed and held up the applications in front of my face.

My stomach tightened. At that moment, I hated him. He'd been using me all along so he could just fill in more blanks on his college applications.

His lip curled up in that smart-alecky way.

Then suddenly, Ms. Burns burst out of the office. "Don't you two have classes to get back to?"

Daniel saluted. "Yes, ma'am. We're on our way."

He marched toward the stairs while I walked the other way, seething with the sting of betrayal.

"So you mean Daniel was using you all along to get a Gold Sword award?" Lindsay said.

I stared at a bowl of apples my mother had just finished photographing. "Apparently."

"Are you sure?"

"Well, he sat there right in front of Ms. Burns this morning and said so. He even took the application."

"Maybe he was just humoring her," Lindsay said.

I grabbed a waxy piece of fruit from the bowl. "He's as fake as the shine on this apple."

"But it really seemed like he was into the whole nonconformity thing."

"Then why did he laugh and hold the applications in front of my face when I questioned him?"

Lindsay shrugged. "I don't know."

I threw the apple back into the bowl. "I'll tell you why. It's because he's just as much of a suck-up as Carly and Kristin and everyone else. He's only out for himself—just like they are." My voice got louder and Lindsay's eyes widened. "You know what?" I said. "Someone's got to take a stand on this. Someone's got to have some integrity. I'm calling Brian right now and telling him I can't go to the prom with him."

Lindsay sat quietly as I punched the numbers on the phone.

"Cougars rule!" Brian's voice mail announced. "Leave a message and I'll call you back."

"Hey, Brian." I tried to sound friendly but firm. "It's Emily. I just wanted to let you know that I really have to go to the alternative prom. A lot of people are counting on me. And . . . it's the right thing to do. I'm sorry I can't go to the regular prom with you. I'm really sorry . . . but . . . if you want to go to the alternative prom with me, that'd be great. Call me if you do and I'll get you a ticket . . . Bye."

I hung up the phone slowly.

Lindsay's eyes were even wider than they'd been when I was ranting. "Wow. I can't believe you just did that."

"Yeah," I said. "Me neither." I grabbed an apple and furiously scrubbed it under running water till the shiny veneer was gone.

"What do you think he'll do?"

I crunched into the apple. "I don't know," I said. "But it's out of my hands now."

Once Lindsay left, I tried to concentrate on my Latin homework, but all I could focus on was an empty feeling I had inside. I'd probably lost any chance I had with Brian. And I'd inadvertently helped Daniel scam Ms. Keenan by doing the right thing for the wrong reasons. I didn't even have conflict to sustain me anymore. Just emptiness.

I stared at my Latin book, but my vision kept blurring from tears. How would it go? *Veni, vidi, flevi*?

I came. I saw. I cried.

NINETEEN

Emily on Her Way

For the rest of the week, I waited for Brian to call. After he'd made his stand about basketball so that Lily could go out with the captain, I thought for a brief moment that he'd go against the team and come with me. But I'd been looking at Brian through crush goggles. He knew his father would never let him quit basketball. Just like I knew my phone wasn't about to ring. He seemed to be avoiding me in person, too, because I never spotted him at school or at home. Although I didn't go out of my way to find him either. Maybe because I didn't want to hear his answer. If he didn't have enough guts to stand up to his parents and his friends and come to the alternative prom with me . . . if he cared more about following the crowd than following his heart, then he wasn't Galahad after all.

In the meantime, I'd also managed to avoid any serious conversation with Daniel by taking the lunch shift with the tickets, while he sold them after school. I vowed I'd never have anything to do with him once the two proms were over. I'd even decided to give up the coeditor position if it was offered to us. The thought of working with him for a full year made me more nauseous than the ride on the Zipper and the *Conga Queen* put together.

By the end of the week, we'd sold six more tickets, making a total of seventeen. It wasn't exactly cause for celebration, but if we counted the donations my parents had gotten for us, we had enough money to put on the two proms.

Two proms. Any girl's dream. Too bad one involved hanging out with my grandmother's peer group and the other meant giving up my dream date.

How could I have been so wrong about everything?

Brian wasn't Galahad.

Daniel wasn't . . . well, Daniel.

And I was never going to take the world by storm.

The least I could do was throw myself into the whole alternative prom. We'd recruited three people to help with the decorations and entertainment: Lindsay, Natalia, and one more unexpected volunteer—Brianna. When Austin found out her parents wouldn't let her go to a hotel after the prom, he dropped her and found another date. I don't know if it was altruism or just plain anger that got her on board, but either way, we decided to bend the rules and let a sophomore join us.

The five of us planned to meet on Friday afternoon to shop for decorations. We had a week left to plan for the two proms—plenty of time when you considered the days we were saving by not shopping for shoes or going to the spa and beauty salon.

We'd all agreed to meet in front of The Party Store, which turned out to be a big mistake.

I got there early and was waiting in my car when Daniel popped up next to my window.

"Hey," he said. "Long time no . . . well, you know. Have you been avoiding me?"

I stared straight ahead.

"Whoa," Daniel said. "I was just kidding, but apparently you're not. What's going on?"

I took a deep breath and faced him. "I don't know. Maybe it has something to do with you being a lying, duplicitous creep."

"Those are some harsh words," Daniel said. "But I do like the 'duplicitous' part—it has a nice ring."

"Figures," I said, sneering.

"Well, now that we've taken care of *why* you're avoiding me, could you tell me exactly what event caused you to come to this erroneous conclusion?"

"Don't try sounding like a lawyer," I said. "You know what you did."

Daniel's face got serious. "No, I really don't."

"Gold Sword award?" I said.

"Yeah, what about it?"

"I thought we were doing the alternative prom for the right reasons, not for the glory of an award or a line on a college application."

"Yeah, that's what I thought, too."

"Then why did you take those papers from Ms. Burns?"

Daniel laughed. "Is *that* what this is all about?"

"Yes, and apparently I don't find it as funny as you do."

"Maybe that's because I have no intention of winning a Gold Sword award."

"Then why did you take the application?"

"What was I going to do? I had to humor her."

"So what did you do with the papers?"

"I threw them away," Daniel said. He pointed to his car where Brianna was sitting inside. "Ask her; she'll tell you."

I looked over at Brianna and then back at Daniel. "Are you telling the truth?"

"I swear on a stack of *Crestview Couriers*."

"Well . . . okay, then I'm not mad at you anymore."

"Did you really think I was serious?" Daniel said.

"Totally."

He made a fake sad face. "I'm hurt."

"You've got to admit you were pretty convincing."

Daniel cocked his head. "I was, wasn't I?" Then he added, "So, we're cool then?"

I nodded. But before I could say anything else, Lindsay and Natalia arrived and we all went inside The Party Store.

"Hey, how about these?" Lindsay yelled down the aisle.

I turned to find her posing in a pirate's hat and eye patch.

"Arrrgh, matey," Daniel said. "That's a fine outfit—"

"But not exactly right for the residents of Mount Saint Mary's," I added.

"Probably not," Daniel said. "I think they'll need the use of both eyes when they're dancing."

Natalia held up a tablecloth with zebras, giraffes, and elephants. "How about a save-the-animals theme?"

I pictured Natalia's posters of animals crammed in cages plastered all over the recreation room at the nursing home. "I don't know," I said. "Let's try to come up with something more festive."

Lindsay and I stayed back a little so I could tell her about Daniel.

"So he really is a good guy after all?" she said.

"Yeah, weird isn't it?" I whispered as we caught up

with Daniel and Brianna.

Daniel had on a grass skirt and lei over his Country Ridge Elementary Jump-a-Thon T-shirt. He was dancing next to Brianna and laughing. "Darn, you caught us," he said. "Friday night is hula night at the Cummings house."

Brianna pushed him with her shoulder. "You're such a nerd," she said with affection. Then she added, "How about Island Adventures?"

I was beginning to think Daniel wasn't the opportunistic jerk I'd made him out to be. Maybe there was something decent underneath that cocky exterior after all.

I turned to Lindsay. "Do you know any island music the residents can dance to?"

She thought for a few seconds. Behind her, Daniel started humming a familiar song.

Lindsay glared at Daniel. "I think I can come up with something better than the theme song from *Gilligan's Island*."

"Okay," I said. "An island theme it is."

After assuring Natalia that there would be no roasting of pigs in the backyard, we picked up some more grass skirts, leis, plates and cups with tropical flower prints, balloons, and other decorations.

I left The Party Store with the sound of Daniel's humming still in my head.

TWENTY

Emily Changes Course

Later, when I was hauling the party stuff out of my car, Brian pulled into his driveway. I still wasn't sure if I'd been avoiding him or he'd been avoiding me all week, so I decided to pretend I didn't see him. I purposely dropped about twenty small bags of balloons on the grass and then proceeded to pick them up one at a time so I could keep looking down. I was tossing yellow balloons into The Party Store bag when Brian's sneakers came into view.

"Haven't seen you in a while," Brian said.

I pointed to the balloons. "Well, you know. I've been busy."

He looked at the bag as if he didn't understand the connection.

I stood and clutched the bag to my chest. "They're decorations," I said, "for the nursing home and the backyard."

He nodded without changing his expression. After a few awkward seconds, he blurted. "Hey, I've got good news."

My heart pounded. Could Brian see it thumping like a cartoon heart, behind the bag of balloons in front of me? Had he chosen me over the regular prom after all?

He went on. "My plan worked."

"What?" I said. "What plan?"

"I told my dad I'd give up basketball if Grams couldn't go on another date and he caved. Now she can see Captain Miguel again."

My heart joined the remaining balloons on the ground. Was that all he had to say? I *was* truly happy for Lily. At least one of us deserved to be with her dream guy. "Great," I repeated, trying to muster some enthusiasm.

"Why don't you go over later," Brian said. "I know she's really excited to talk about it with someone. And, you know, I don't think I'm the right person." He smiled that smile of his, the one that made his eyes sparkle like the morning sun on the Intracoastal. "And I think she wants to ask you something."

Brian picked up the last balloon and handed it to me. "My parents are going out and I've got a poker game at Austin's so she'll really be happy to see you."

He paused. "I'm really sorry about the whole prom thing. But I just have to go to the real one. The team is counting on me. My dad's real excited about the limo and my mom can't wait to see me in a tux. So . . . I had to ask Brandy to go with me. I really wish it was you. But, you know, I couldn't disappoint my parents after all the plans they've made."

And just like that, it was over. The Boy Next Door was now just the boy next door.

"I'm afraid my family isn't happy with us these days," Lily said. She poured me a cup of her now familiar green tea.

The feeling was pretty mutual.

"I hope you're not too upset about the prom," Lily said. "Brian explained it all to me." She offered me a blueberry muffin. "I'm sorry, dear, but Brian isn't like us."

"Us?" I said through a mouthful of muffin.

"You can't expect him to go against the crowd. He just wasn't raised that way."

I wanted to shout, *Neither was I.* My dad's an accountant and my mother takes pictures of food. Whoopee! Where's the daring originality there? But then I remembered the whole closing-the-draft-board story and my mother's deferred dream of taking pictures to save the environment. Deep down, they *were* activists.

"He's my grandson and I love him very much, but . . . he's still a bit immature. He's like those silly snow globes his parents collect, stuck inside with everyone else. He isn't ready to break out yet . . . maybe he never will be."

I felt like a fraud. I'd *wanted* to go to the regular prom with Brian. Plans just got carried away. "I don't know if I'm any different," I confessed. "The alternative prom came about by accident—it wasn't anything I really planned."

"That's what proves your character," Lily said. "When things got out of hand, you rose to the occasion. You could have backed out and gone to the prom with Brian. But you didn't. You made the right choice. It's all in the choices, my dear."

"But we only got seventeen people together," I said. "I haven't made that much difference."

"Oh, but you have, dear. You've set an example. And look at all those people in the nursing home you'll be helping."

"Do you really think a prom will help them?"

Lily's eyes brightened. "It's like Captain Miguel says, 'Anything you can do to make the world a more beautiful place is worth trying.' It's the little gestures, my dear. The little gestures that make other people smile, even for just a short time."

I nodded. "Maybe you're right."

Lily took a sip of tea and sat back in her chair. "And

now I have a favor to ask you."

I hoped it didn't involve the delivery of any more notes. My matchmaking days were so over.

"Next Saturday night Captain Miguel is taking me for a cruise on the *Conga Queen*." Lily brought her hand to her forehead in a salute. "I'm going to be his first mate."

"So, you had a good time?"

"Oh, yes, lovely," Lily said. She leaned toward me and continued. "But since I won't be able to dance for the *Conga Queen* and the other boats next Saturday night, I'd like you to take over for me."

"What?" She *had* to be joking.

"Take over for me and dance for the boats," Lily said as if it was the most normal thing in the world.

"But I don't know how to dance."

Lily laughed. "Of course you do. Everyone knows how to dance."

"No," I argued. "I honestly don't. I was kicked out of ballet classes for not being able to point my toes the right way."

"Nonsense, dear," Lily said. "It won't matter what you look like. Just dance from within. Dance from your heart." Her eyes pleaded with me. "I'll show you some easy steps to do."

"No, really," I said. "I can't."

"Dear," Lily said. "It's not just about the dancing. It's about the freedom. Breaking away from the humdrum. Getting out of the snow globe."

"But I'll make a fool of myself."

"Nonsense. Fools refuse to try something new."

I thought about Brian and his crowd waiting for the limo at his house. What if the limo came late and everyone saw me dancing?

And there was no way I could hide from Daniel and everyone at the alternative prom.

"Dear, do you want to be like those Clausen girls and everyone else? Or do you want to *dance*?"

Lily sure knew which buttons to press.

But the way she said the word *dance*, I knew she meant more than just doing steps. It wasn't about entertaining the ships. It was about living, living in such a way that you didn't care what people thought.

It was about not answering to the Harringtons or Crestview Prep or anyone but yourself. It was about being true to who you were.

It all made sense. I wasn't like those other girls. I had goals. Ambition. I was going to take the world by storm someday.

Maybe this was a start.

"You want me to dance?" I said. "I'll rock the whole Intracoastal."

TWENTY-ONE

Emily Grows in Strength

For the whole next week, it seemed all anyone talked about was their preprom, prom, and postprom plans. Meanwhile, Daniel and I were trying to figure out how we could coordinate the "senior" prom at Mount Saint Mary's during the day, and then pick up the food and decorate for the junior prom in my backyard at night.

Because of the strict schedule at Mount Saint Mary's, the nursing home prom would be held between lunch and dinner in the recreation room. Frances said she'd take care of the snacks since so many residents had dietary restrictions.

We all arrived at the nursing home around noon. Daniel brought a helium tank for the balloons. And

Brianna was right behind him with a gallon of water in each hand and some fishing line under her arm.

"Huh?" I said. Water and fishing line did not seem conducive to festive partying—even for senior citizens.

"It's for a balloon archway," Brianna said. She set a gallon of water on each side of the doorway to the recreation room and tied the ends of the fishing line to the handles. Then she blew up an orange balloon and attached it to the fishing line. Then, whoosh! The balloon rose to the ceiling, taking the fishing line with it. "Each time you tie a balloon on the string, it rises. Soon you have a whole archway of balloons."

"Cool," Lindsay said. "Can I try?" She gave a yellow balloon a squirt of helium, attached it, and then watched it ascend. Lindsay, Daniel, and I formed an assembly line to do the arch, while Brianna and Natalia hung shiny blue streamers over the windows to look like waterfalls. Frances came in and offered us the use of two palm trees in the lobby, so Daniel went out and got those, too.

With the trees, the archway, the fake waterfalls, and the tropical-print tablecloths and napkins, the rec room was starting to look pretty islandy. We dimmed the lights so it wouldn't look like afternoon. Lindsay took her place at the piano and the rest of us greeted the residents with shouts of "Aloha" and tossed leis around their necks and pinned grass skirts over their clothes.

Lindsay had picked out some tunes from Broadway shows like *South Pacific* and *Once on This Island* and started playing. One of the older men grabbed Natalia's hand and spun her around. I thought she was going to haul off and slap him, but she actually started dancing with him. Maybe she figured it was a captive audience for her antibeef speech.

Brianna helped with drinks and cookies, and Daniel and I waited by the archway in case anyone else came in late. Some of the residents began to pair up and sway together to the music. Since there weren't as many men, some of the women danced with each other.

"They look pretty happy," I said.

Daniel smiled and then walked toward a man sitting alone in a chair, staring off into space. I couldn't hear what they were saying, but I watched their exchange. After a minute, Daniel picked a pink flower out of one of the centerpieces, handed it to the man, and said something else before coming back to me.

"What was that all about?" I said.

"He wanted to ask that woman over there to dance, but he was too shy."

She was a petite woman with curly gray hair and bright eyes. The man handed her the flower. She stuck it in the buttonhole of her blouse, and they began to dance.

"You're quite the matchmaker," I told Daniel.

His lip curled up on the end, but it didn't seem so obnoxious this time. "I just told him I thought she'd love to dance with him, but she was probably shy, too. . . . and that the flower wouldn't hurt."

The two of them swayed together in the middle of the rec room. "I guess you called it right."

Daniel smiled again. This time the lip curl almost looked cute. "So how about you?" he said. "Wanna dance?"

I recognized the song from when Crestview put on *South Pacific*. It was "Some Enchanted Evening." I felt Daniel's fingers lightly touching my back as we stepped from side to side with the music. Neither of us really knew how to do that kind of dancing. What was it my grandfather called it, the fox-trot? The words played inside my head . . . something about finding a stranger in a crowded room.

"I hope you won't mind sharing the editor position next year," Daniel said.

I looked up at him and smelled his woodsy-scented cologne. "Not unless you do."

Daniel laughed. "I was the one who suggested to Ms. Keenan that she pick two editors. At first she tried to pair me up with Carly for the prom story, but I asked if we could pair up instead."

I didn't know what to say.

"I read a story in the newspaper about these four

guys who made a pact during their freshman year that no one would try to get ahead of the others by taking extra AP classes or anything else," Daniel continued. "They were friends and they were all smart, so they figured they'd cooperate with each other instead of competing for valedictorian. I liked their style."

Daniel pulled me closer to him. A tingling ran down my arms and legs. It wasn't a nervous tingle like the kind I'd felt with Brian. It was warmer, like the kind you feel on Christmas morning when your whole family's around you.

For the rest of the afternoon I didn't know what to make of Daniel's confession. Had we not been competing all along? Who was this person?

I watched as he danced with the elderly women, twirling them and dipping them till they were giddy. He even danced with a woman in a wheelchair.

The prom went by quickly—Frances had said a couple of hours would be enough for most of the residents and she was right. By the time Natalia convinced Lindsay to ditch the island music and play the bunny hop, only a few joined in.

"This is the nicest thing anyone has ever done for us," the tiny woman with the gray hair and the pink flower in her buttonhole said on her way out of the rec room. Others thanked us and said they hoped we'd come to see them again. Lily had been right. A small gesture could go a long way.

Lindsay played the theme song to *Gilligan's Island* while the rest of us cleaned up. Daniel and I reached for one of the flowered centerpieces at the same time. "You take it," he said. I put it in the cardboard box, and then looked up at him and smiled. "One prom down. One more to go."

TWENTY-TWO

Emily Rocks South Florida

After a short rest and shower, I got myself ready for Prom No. 2. It had seemed a little hypocritical to buy a new outfit, so I wore my newest pair of jeans and a top Lindsay had given me. It was a shirt from the play *Wicked*, with the words DEFY GRAVITY across the front. I'd worn it only once before and Brandy and Randy had pointed at it and asked if it was talking about my boobs.

Daniel had dropped Brianna off before he went to pick up the food. She joined me in the backyard to set up the tables. I tried to ignore the commotion going on at the Harrington house. Cars pulling up. The rustle of expensive gowns. The music out by the pool where parents yelled "Smile" and snapped pictures of their kids against the backdrop of the setting sun on the water. Brianna and I shook a bright floral tablecloth in the air and smoothed it over a table under the tent.

"Are you okay about not going to the prom?" I asked.

"Yeah, I'm over it now," she said. "How about you?"

"So over it," I said.

I ripped open the plastic cover of a second paper tablecloth. "I'd much rather be here."

Brianna smiled. "You know, I would have disagreed with you a few weeks ago. But after Austin dumped me, I didn't miss that crowd at all. They don't have any more fun than anyone else; they just have better PR about it."

"What do you mean?"

"Have you ever noticed how all they talk about is what a great time they had the *last* time they were all together? In the cafeteria and in the halls, even at parties, they're always talking about the cool thing they did before. It would be like if you and Daniel had only *talked* about doing the alternative prom but never actually did it."

I was thinking about what Brianna said when my brother came running to announce that Daniel and Lindsay had arrived with the food. We all helped carry sodas and platters of food to the backyard. After several trips back and forth, Daniel and I were alone at the car with only a couple of platters left.

He looked at my shirt. "From *Wicked*, right?"

I nodded and pointed to his—a T-shirt with a tux painted on the front. "From the thrift store, right?"

"Right," Daniel said. Then he reached into the front seat of his car, pulled out one long-stemmed pink rose, and handed it to me. "This is for you. I didn't think you'd want a corsage since it would kind of go against our whole anti-expensive-prom thing. But I know how you had to give up your date with Harrington and . . ." He stopped in mid-sentence as if he hadn't rehearsed the rest of the speech.

I took the rose, which hadn't fully opened yet, and inhaled the sweet scent. My eyes met Daniel's and I suddenly wanted to tell him everything. All about how I'd wanted to get revenge on Brandy. How I'd wanted to beat him out of the editor in chief position. About how I was wrong about Brian. Wrong about lots of things.

But just as I started to tell him, as if breaking a spell, a giant silver Hummer pulled in front of the Harringtons' house. Daniel turned to get a look and scowled. "Can you spell conspicuous consumption?"

I held onto the rose and balanced a tray of fried bananas with my free hand. Squeals erupted from next door and everyone rushed to see the limo. Parents followed with their cameras. I was about to take my rose and the platter to the backyard when I heard my name. I spun around to find Brian, looking hotter than ever in a black tux with a bright red cummerbund. He strolled toward Daniel and me. Daniel grunted something, then took my platter and walked away.

"Hey," I said, trying to sound casual. "How are you doing?"

Brian did the trademark nod and repeated, "Doin' well. Doin' well." Then he added. "I just wanted to say thanks for being so understanding about the prom and for telling Grams you'd dance for her."

"Sure," I said.

Brian gestured toward the backyard and then at me. "So, how are you doin'?"

"Doin' good," I said. "Doin'—"

"Br-i-i-ian." Brandy Clausen's whine suddenly pierced the air. She stretched out the *I* so that somehow even Brian's name would be all about her. "I need you next to me for the picture."

Brian rolled his eyes.

Brandy called out again. Brian turned and waved to her. "Guess I'd better go," he said. "See you?"

"Sure." I walked backward, away from him, clutching my rose in one hand and waving with the other. I watched him pose next to Brandy, in her shiny red dress. I expected to feel a pang of jealousy, and was surprised when I didn't.

Back in the kitchen, my mother had created her famous punch with rainbow sherbet, pineapple, and maraschino cherries, and a picture-perfect watermelon filled with fruit. I admired her work and then asked for a vase for the rose.

"It's from Daniel," I said. "In lieu of a corsage. It's sort of a pity rose."

My mother laughed. "I'm pretty sure there's no such thing as a pity rose." She put it in a vase and handed it to me. "You'd better go," she said.

When I went back outside, everyone was already digging into the food and Brianna was playing DJ.

I glanced at my watch. Almost time.

A horn sounded and I looked out at the water to find the *Conga Queen* in the distance. I grabbed the CD I'd rehearsed with and gave it to Brianna. She turned up the volume and everyone turned to see why John Mayer's "No Such Thing" was suddenly blaring.

The *Conga Queen* shot a beam of light into the yard. I stepped into it and began to move. I started with the strut that Lily taught me. How did it go? One, two, three, four.

Then the kicks. Up and down. Up and down.

Then what was that step called? Grapevine. Cross front, side, back, side.

The boat drew closer, and I could see Lily and the captain with their matching hats. Lily saluted and the captain blew the horn again. I waved and then flung my arms to the sides.

My heart began to race.

I spun again and again. Turning, twirling. My arms reaching to the sky. Dancing from deep down the way Lily had described.

I was unaware of anyone around me. And then all of a sudden Daniel was by my side. I stopped to look at him and stumbled. He caught me in his arms.

"Are you okay?" he asked.

I nodded. "How about you? How are you doing?"

"Good," he said. "Pretty darn good."

Wrapped in a circle of light from the *Conga Queen*, it suddenly hit me:

Doing good was a lot different than doing well.

How had I not realized that all these months?

I stayed in Daniel's arms, inhaling his familiar scent.

We began dancing together, side by side. Natalia and Lindsay joined us and the others followed. Suddenly we were all doing the bunny hop to John Mayer. I could feel the truth of the lyrics. No prom kings or drama queens here. We were all dancing outside the lines and it didn't matter.

"Are you sorry you didn't go to the real prom?" Daniel yelled over the music.

"No!" I shouted, surprised at how easily it came out.

Daniel grabbed me by the waist. I looked into his

eyes, startled. I remembered the first time I'd seen Lindsay play Chopin's "Fantaisie Impromptu." I knew I was looking at some secret part of her, way down deep, that I'd never seen before. That was how I felt when I was staring into Daniel's eyes.

He smiled and then picked me up and spun me around and around and around. The world seemed to be spinning along in perfect sync when the words came to me: *Veni, vidi* . . . ah, forget Latin . . .

I came.

I saw.

I *rocked*.

Acknowledgments

Many, many thanks go to:

My editor, Tara Weikum, for always encouraging me to dig deeper and for understanding my work almost better than I do. I am a lucky writer to have her at the helm.

My agent, Steven Chudney, for his speedy responses and advice, and for taking care of everything that has to do with numbers.

Erica Sussman and everyone else behind the scenes at HarperCollins who has worked so hard to put this book together and to place it in the hands of readers.

Julie Arpin, Kathy Macdonald, and Gloria Rothstein for letting me brainstorm, whine, and complain on an almost daily basis without ever letting on that I can be most annoying.

Phyllis Laszlo for introducing me to great literature and teaching me that my ideas were worthy enough to jot down in the margins of my books.

Joyce Sweeney for starting me off on this journey and for getting together two fabulous critique groups that have provided me with both their ideas and enthusiasm. Thanks to all of you for your support.

Alex Flinn, E. Lockhart, Nancy Werlin, Lara Zeises, and the entire cyber community of writers for their willingness to share their knowledge of both writing and publishing.

All of my friends and family members who continually support what I'm doing in so many ways. I hope you all know who you are.

Daniel Iden for lending me his first name and his former taste in T-shirts and Brett Kushner for contributing his humor back in our carpool days. I miss those times.

My son, Blaise, for the constant jokes, and I do mean constant, and for always keeping me company.

My daughter, Siena, for her inspiration and willingness to read every word I write.

My husband, Stephen, for his love and support, but mostly for never complaining about eating take-out food or having to step over the piles in the study.

And, lastly, thanks go to the anonymous old man, who has probably since passed on, whom I saw dancing in his backyard more than twenty years ago. His joie de vivre and desire to make the world more beautiful by giving everyone who sailed the Intracoastal a laugh was an inspiration. I hope he's dancing in heaven.